Aakhir and Other Stories

Aakhir and Other Stories

ABU SIDDIK

AUTHORSPRESS

Worldwide Circulation through Authorspress Global Network
First Published in 2022
by
Authorspress
Q-2A Hauz Khas Enclave, New Delhi-110 016 (India)
Phone: (0) 9818049852
E-mail: authorspressgroup@gmail.com
Website: www.authorspressbooks.com

Aakhir and Other Stories

ISBN 978-93-5529-194-3

Printed in India at Thomson Press (India) Limited

Dedicated to
The toilers of our time

I love short stories because I believe they are the way we live. They are what our friends tell us, in their pain and joy, their passion and rage, their yearning and their cry against injustice.

– Andre Dubus (1936-1999)

ACKNOWLEDGEMENTS

All the poor people of our land from whom I have learnt the stories of victory and defeat.

CONTENTS

1

A MAID UNDER CORONA-CLOUD

A 2020 March morning at a banker's house in a suburban town in West Bengal.

The world is shaken with the spread of deadly, highly contagious corona virus. Over one lakh fifty thousand people of different nationalities are reported to have been infected across the globe, and thousands have died in its wake. Countries have shut down malls, multiplexes, public gatherings. Checks, screenings, and quarantine facilities are being installed at airports, ports, borderlines. Citizens are warned, barred from travelling to foreign countries. Schools, colleges, offices across the country are partially closed for a fortnight. Business houses have ordered workers to work from home. Religious places are also closed to avoid congregation.

People are scary. They prefer to be confined within four walls. Streets are deserted. Trains, buses run irregularly and especially for emergency services. The town is cheerless. Parks, tea shops and restaurants are closed.

"Mala, go straight to basin, take hand wash and clean hands first," the mistress of the house yawns and orders while unlocking the door.

"Madam, daily I do," Mala retorts with a proud look.

Mala fastens her sari and begins to lather hands, and the mistress standing like a stone watches her. "Soiled sari…dirty street…germs coated …" she mutters with a reproachful look.

"Soap hands well, take a good drop again. Leave your misery at home?" mistress chides.

Mala washes hands thrice and then hurries to washing place, takes dishes, plates, cups, saucepans, tumblers, etc. one by one and starts washing. Moon, a one year healthy child, is nestled asleep in bed. A fan is slowly moving overhead.

Lady of the house is in sportswear. She stretches legs, raises hands, spins body, lies long, and takes deep breath.

Master is in a private bank. He is busy before laptop. Today is a rose day! A huge project is fixed to be sanctioned. He is tensed and his eyes glued to the magic figures. "A large fish is waddling in clean lake, net is already cast. Only I have to tighten the noose," the middle aged, ruddy, master giggles and sips tea with sounds of elation.

A sneeze is heard in the wash place. It is so abrupt and unexpected. The banker rubs tip of his sharp nose. He is perturbed. Madam is wary. She runs to Mala.

"Are you suffering from cold?" panicky she asks.

"No, madam, yesterday I was on fast and in the evening I took bath in the river," she soberly says without turning her head.

"Oh, have you no kerchief? Haven't you covered mouth, nose with hands?" Madam looks anxious and baffled.

"I never do," Mala casually put.

"You poor folks have no sense! Don't you know corona virus is in our corner? One died in our neighbouring state! Don't you watch T.V.? Stand there. I give you a bucket of boiling water. Wash the utensils again." She hurries to gizzard-tap.

Mala works in seven houses. This is her first turn. One hour is allotted to each. If she is late other houses will burn her alive. The whole day will be series shows of abuse and harsh hails! Moreover, she has not yet touched clothes. Floor remains to be mopped yet.

"Madam, I'm in hurry. I can't wash again," Mala gathers courage and says.

"What? You sneeze! You spread germs! And am I to kill them?" shouts the mistress in rage.

Mala wears a sad face, becomes subdued, fights with the dishes and hastily washes them again.

Meantime master has shut down his laptop. He is readying for brush, shave, and bath. Body, hairy, bare, a napkin tied round his round neck, he begins to brush. Then he gurgles for five minutes. When finished, he dictates Mala to carefully and slowly clean the corners, window sills, railings with dettol-water.

Mala hears and nods without a word. She is sour. She thinks of the bad tempered lone old man who will dance in fire if she is late even by a minute.

After washing the dishes Mala starts to rinse a hill of saris, pajamas, pants, shirts, underwears, socks, curtains, pillow covers, bed sheets, etc. Her face is rained with sweat. She feels cold. Her lips parched. Her head reels.

"Mala, rinse collars of shirts charily. Your dada don't like a soiled collar. Make it clean as snow," mistress demands. And next she is seen sipping an energetic health drink, morning paper on tea table staring at her with a bold cap "Corono Virus

Spreads Tentacles Across India; 114 Infected, Mask Unavailable."

"Mala," she briskly sides aside the mug to the edge of the table and exhorts; "tomorrow you must come with your mask." It is taking shape of a pandemic. She cautiously flips the pages and she cannot believe her eyes. Pages after pages are filled with the same news of corona and countries after countries are being affected afresh. It is 2020. Tremendous progress we have made in medical sciences. Madam strives to allay her fear by such positive thoughts. But next she looks worried. Aged and children are most vulnerable. And her Moon is just a bundle of flesh! She rushes to the basin, washes her hands, sanitizes herself and goes to her daughter's bed and caresses her head with a humming and asks gods for blessings.

Mala, however, is fatigued in brushing, rinsing, and wringing the clothes. Her lean hands and bow legs are in a soapy puddle. Madam's warning has no bearings on her. Drudgery of remaining six houses occupies her perturbed mind.

Two nubile daughters at home! Husband drunkard! Disease and death cannot maim her fragile limbs.

❖❖❖

2

A MAN OF BARISAL

The train was not running. It halted almost for two hours at a nameless sleepy station. The passengers were impatient. They were getting late, and they abused all – from Railway minister to gang man, and comments like, 'India is destroyed,' 'All are corrupts,' 'Nothing bright will happen here' and many mores were rampant. The commentators included the respectable senior citizens, service men, job aspirant youths, and hawkers. Children were crying, and people queued before toilets. Working women were chattering, the elegant and stylish ones measured beauty by their hand bag mirrors, and the college girls facebooking, chatting, viewing YouTube, playing games. And the poor housewives sat dolefully with vacant looks. The hawkers had a hay day. And the beggars, the real and the fake, the old and the young, men and women, the third genders, and ah…the poor blind singers with bamboo flutes, harmoniums, and ektaras – all entertained and mesmerized the passengers. Everybody was speaking everything, no hearers. And it was such a happy journey.

"Uncle, where are you going?" A newly married man of Kankinara asked. The young man was accompanied by his nagging and talkative wife. She was of mediocre beauty, and it seemed she was the single daughter of a service man. And she pestered his husband for *mumfuli*, pieces of cheap handicrafts hawkers selling, *jhaal muri*.

"Going to Kolkata," and the man continued, "My sons all lived in the city. I'm a retired man. No work at home and they are calling me for many months. So I decide to air with them for a week."

The man was short and black with a bulging belly. He was partially bald. A few strands of grey hair, coloured yellowish for the visit, made a futile effort to cover the edges of his flat head. The thick spectacled man had leather chappals, and wore a formal shirt and pants, all newly tailored, and neatly screeched. He put on a grey half sweater, and his grey muffler was tied to his short neck. He spoke softly. He was over seventy, and had served some offices of Bengal. He was a gourmet, and his bulging belly was a testimony to it.

"Are you a *bangal*, a man from Bangladesh I mean?" The young man casually asked.

"Why?" The retiree gentleman said in a voice that I understand that he was offended and hurt.

"No, nothing in particular," the young man spoke gently, and it was obvious that he was a bit repentant for his casual remark. "Don't take it serously, uncle. You know we are called *ghoti* and the bangals are called *bati*. And your articulation is somewhat differs from us. That's why, I put it. And if you get hurt, I'm sorry."

"No, no." He smiled mildly, and said, "Originally I'm from Bangladesh. You're right."

The train did not move an inch. Most of the passengers left their coaches, and loitering around the station. No tea stall, no drinking water, only some brick made benches etched with chalks by children stared at us indifferently. Afternoon sun glowed, and the open fields and the trees looked resplendent. The sky was clear blue. By one side of the station a path went to the village. On the other side, tea gardens with lush green foliages stretched miles after miles. The plants were shredded so evenly, that it seemed that the entire garden is a bed covered with a thick green blanket. The rain trees dotted the bagan, and their trunks were white or yellow ringed. Passengers went to the sides of the bagan, and urinated open. Some smoked, some chewed betel nuts, and others took tobacco, ghutkha, paan parag.

Our coach was almost empty. A moment of silence crossed us. The man then began with his volition, "It was 1966 or 1967, before the creation of Bangladesh. Razakars plundered, looted us, torched Hindu houses, and spoilt our women. It was a terrible time, anarchy ran loose. Our Muslim neighbours were good, and they promised us protection. But our grandfathers and parents were terribly shaken. My father first declined to come to India. But when the entire Hindu relatives and neighbours left our village, my father could not keep courage to stay there. But he was at pains to leave his motherland, leaving all the farm lands and property. But who wanted to be butchered by the Pakistani assailants. They were not men, all barbaric and cruel to the core. And so we left our rivers, lands, playing fields, schools, friends, and neighbours. And coming to India, in those days, you know, was terribly hard."

The man scratched his head, and removed his glass. He unzipped his bag, and took a bottle of water to drink. He was speaking of his own, not with particular force. His words were all desultory, and it seemed he didn't believe in the power of words' exactitudes.

"Then what?" the young man took much interest in him, and pursued him to proceed.

"Oh..." The old man sighed, and coughed dryly. He tied the muffler more tightly around his neck. He brushed his demure eyes with his slackened hands, and he wiped the dark patches on his face with a white kerchief, and it got sullied. His friend aged the same, in dhoti and panjabi and wrapped in a milk white saal sat beside him still. He did not utter a word. And when his friend talked, he looked at outside scenes through the window. His cheeks were sunk, and he lost two or three upper teeth. He was lean and tall, and his head was covered with thick black and white hair. His eyes were sharp, and now and then he tried to read a Bengali daily. All I watch from my side upper birth.

The man began again with no jest. He was utterly casual and careless in his approach, as if he knew the entire world, and the young man was a novice. "The time was hard. We were not mature enough. We took shelter at a relative's house near Dum Dum. We were four brothers and three sisters. We fled so quickly. We had no time to sell our lands. We came here with only hands and legs. Father couldn't sleep. But my mother was very strong. She never surrendered to the hardships and calamities. With grace and smile she bore all, and brought up us. At teenage we worked in shoe stores, masonry, even in farming lands. We had been coolies and hawkers too. Then slowly with the help of a close relative father somehow managed to buy a plot and we shifted there. It was in Ashoke Nagar. It was a deep forest. We lived on planking huts. Collegepara was then a fearful place. At day tigers, elephants, cheetahs, bisons roamed freely. There were two ghoti (men originally of West Bengal) huts, two brothers – Laxmikanta and Kalikanta living in the forest. They were zamindars, and had huge lands. But they were lazy people. They loved to eat and sleep. They were not educated. And many

Hindus day after day rushed to Bengal from Bangladesh, and they made colonies in Jadavpur, Belghoria, Gharia, Naihati, and Ranaghat and in many more places. Our great Comrade Jyoti Basu supported our cause. And I myself built two colonies, and two schools at Ashoke Nagar."

He stopped for a while, and took out a square squat plastic container, full of tablets, capsules, homeopathic files. He took two capsules and a tablet, and drank together all, and yawned long.

"How did it happen all?" The young man asked. His wife was dozing, and kept her head leaning on his left shoulder. She was not snoring, but her lips were apart. The man's friend sat still, now he changed his posture, and on a reclined and relaxed mood reading a column. There was special expression on his face. It was somewhat grim and dark. Possibly the column was one of accident, rape or corruption. And with it he was not obviously happy. And he seemed to be burdened a bit. He then turned the page, as if to relieve him, and began to read the obituary column or so.

The man again belched, and began, "Besides the zamindars, there were many peasants who had lands, but were perennially poor. Food they had, but other articles like utensils, umbrellas, torches, etc. were borrowed by them from the men of East Bengal refugees, who in meantime was recovering from their wounds of uprootedness, not all but some of them. The poor peasants borrowed, but could not repay. And the interest got multiplied day by day. And to repay the traders they sold lands at throw away prices, and often free of cost. This way many ghoti peasants lost their lands, and uprooted men of erstwhile East Pakistan built colonies there. All happened before my own eyes. What a change? Now could you buy a two kattha plot in Jadavpur? World famous university was built, hospitals, nursing homes, luxury bazaars, and sophisticated, rich skyscrapers all."

He said at a stretch. And I couldn't understand whether he was a happy man or not. His children were all established in Kolkata. One was doctor, one lawyer, and the younger was a wholesaler of automobile parts. His one daughter lived in Berlin. His son-in-law was an I. T. professional posted there. He visited twenty countries, a truly cosmopolitan.

"Do you still visit Bangladesh? Any nostalgia for your land of birth?" The young man asked and checked his android set for new message.

The man continued with the same casualness, and said, "Two or three times I visited my village at Barisal. Some relatives are still living there. On the occasions of marriage and death they call us, and we attend. Not always possible. So much change. At my first visit I was quite puzzled. The villages, the roads, the bazaars, the lands, the ponds – everything was changed. The old people died all, and the younger ones didn't know me. But all were so cordial and friendly that I felt home at Bangladesh. I heard from my father that it would take three days to reach Dhaka from Khulna. First people would have to come from Khulna to Barisal by boats, and then from Barisal to Dhaka they went by big vessels. Now it would take merely five hours from a man of Khulna to reach to Dhaka. And Barisal would remain under water for six months. Rains poured and poured, and flooded the entire country. But we were habituated with it, and we were ready to deal with that. We had boats, and fishes were plenty. And taste! Ah! Fish here all cultivated, had no taste!"

His mouth became watery, and eyes bright. "Like the ghoti we did never buy fish. In Bangladesh buying fish was such a joy.

Affluent people took a coolie before entering the bazaar. He would buy then at least nine or ten varieties of fish – hilsha, tangra, koi, pabda, chingri, singhi, etc. We didn't eat *baata* and *kaata* (pieces of carp and ruhi) so common here. And for fish only he would spend three to four thousands. Not all, not the poor, of course. The man went before, followed by his coolie with a *dali* (basket) on his head. Whatever he saw, he bought and the coolie kept it on the dali, and carried on behind. We loved to eat, and our time was spent to cook all the dishes. And we are rightly called "*mache vate bangali*" (A Bengalee could not live without fish and rice. Ha ha ha..."

The train didn't move. Already an hour and a half passed. People getting frustrated, and some hurling choicest expletives at authorities, and the cooler ones didn't mind at all. They stuck head phones to ears, and watching their favourite movies, reality shows, heores and heroins, cricket stars, latest fads, and their faces were expressionless. The children were running from one end to the other, and the elders were dozing peacefully. A few were sleeping on the upper berths and snoring loudly.

"How are the hindus living there?" The young man asked, and it seemed he was seriously concerned with the issue of Hindu persecution in Bangladesh. And the young man had a fixed view to the hot issue.

"Hasina is good. Hindus love her, and she is trying her best for the safety of our people. And do you know over ten thousand idols of Maa Durga have been worshipped, and celebrated, and Hasina herself took every care for their peaceful immersion. Police this year had done excellent job as well. No disturbance."

He stopped, and took a pinch of snuff from a small box hidden in his hand bag. The bag also had a box of betel leaves, pieces of betel nuts, and other spices needed for paan, a pouch of tobacco, and the case for his spectacles.

The young man was not convinced, and said ruefully, "Muslims here are in *bahal tabiyote* (going fine). If Pakistan wins, the people of Rajabazaar burst crackers, and Mamata Banerjee appeasing them." His face was blight with pathos and anger, and it betrayed his sordidness.

The man supported him, and nodded his head as a token of consent to the young man's arguments.

"Huh…" He looked thoughtful. He wiped his eyes with the fingers of his left hand, and said, "Hasina is right, but if Khaleda Zia voted to power, the Hindus will be butchered." Actually the man used a Bengali term '*kachukata*' which roughly means butchering.

The signal turned green, and the passengers all huddled back to their seats and coaches. The train shook, and began to move. The platform was deserted again, and the lonely station master waved at the dutiful TTEs.

❖❖❖

3

A SABJIWALI

During my stay at Andul, a village in the district of Howrah, I used to buy vegetables from a middle aged woman, a sabjiwali. She was fat and black with a floppy face and a snub nose. She was not too short, and had huge uncombed black hair dangling to the waist. Her neck, nose and ears were bare. I never saw her smiling, always in a dark and casual mood. She wore a printed sari, and a loosc blouse. Her slippers were kept behind her back, and she sat cross legged on a plastic sack. Whether it was sun or shower, she never missed a day to come to the bazaar. Her buyers were all office goers, and she came early morning to serve them. She sold all sorts of vegetables – spinach, brinjal, purble, banana, cauliflower, cabbage, carrot, turnip, tomato, green beans, capsicum, mocha, lemon, gourd, pumpkin, radish, etc. She sat at the left entry corner of the bazaar. She also kept deshi eggs of hens and ducks. I daily cycled, and made some quick buys from her, and came back home as usual. One such morning I saw her weeping in secret, and the old woman beside her tried to soothe her with words of sympathy and love.

I was a regular, and eyeing me, she tried hard to stop her sobbing, and asked my items for the day. I nimbly asked, "Is anything serious in your family, masi? Why are you crying?"

She looked full at me, and hesitated first. Then for what, I could not tell, she confided, "*Beta*, (son), what can I tell? My son-in-law a month ago has brought home a *randi* (a bad woman). What will happen to my daughter now?" And she began to sob again. She was wiping her eyes and the tip of her nose with the end of her faded sari.

"Where have you married your daughter?" I indulgently put.

"Sankrail. Beta, we could not understand the family. A distant relative brought the relation first. We first decided not to give Shibani to any boy. The Madhymik pariksha was ahead. But they pestered so much for my daughter's hand, and we changed our mind. The boy worked in a Marwari gadi at Barabazaar. He earned Rs. 10000 per month. So what's bad? We thought. Moreover, if Shibani gets admitted in college then to find an educated groom would be more difficult. Things were so quickly arranged, and the marriage was done in a month. We arranged band party, and all the villagers dined. She was my only daughter, you know."

"Where is your daughter now?"

Seemingly enraged, the old toothless woman asked my whereabouts. Satisfied with my verified details and open nature, she smiled, and her toothless gums I saw. She had sharp features, skin whitish but wrinkled, and cheeks sunk deep, nose sharp. She was neatly dressed with a white sari, and she seemed a woman of respect and grace with life's ripe certitudes.

"I bought her home. My dadu (grandson) was only of one year and half. The child was so sweet and cute! Children quarrelled to snatch him from Shibani's lap, and they made him see the birds, cats, dogs, cows, goats, and sheep. My dadu smiled, and waddled to catch them." The woman laughed, but soon his face was covered with pallor of ash. She took the water bottle, poured a little water on her head, and she began to thump her head again and again.

A gentleman came for vegetables. He had two bags, one small for fish, and the other for vegetables. He came running to the masi. I stood aside. He bought cucumbers, carrots, beans, and capsicums, and paid her, and looked at me and my bicycle with a look of sneer, and muttered something. It seemed he abused, but whom I didn't know. And hurriedly he went. He was apparently white with the thought of his wife's beatings if he got late.

"Is your daughter beautiful like you?" I casually suggested.

She broadened her eyes in astonishment, and made such a gesture that I gulped my words back, and bit my tongue. My estimate was a blow to her. She thought her daughter a beauty queen. She raised her hands, straightened her sari along her body, and became extremely energetic. Her voice was loud, and the people passing by the way stopped a while and looked close at her. I was flabbergasted. She claimed raising her right hand over her head, "Huh…taller more than you. And she is fair like her father, and has a robust body. She can pull you up by hand. Uhu...such is Shibani's *fikar* (figure)." She stared at me; her face twisted, and she began to size the vegetables, threw the rotten ones out, and sprinkled water on the dried ones. Then she sat silent on the dusty sack, and an old tea-boy brought a cup of tea for her. She offered me a cup from the old-boy but I declined politely.

"So, what you are going to do with your daughter? She had a son, and remarriage would be difficult." I opined in a sympathetic undertone.

"Na, na. We are not thinking of that. Ha, she is just seventeen. Remarriage is not the problem. Many bachelors stand on one leg to snatch her." She scratched her head, poking finger into her thick jabbed hair.

"So, you couldn't complain to the police. You gave Shibani's marriage at underage. If police knew it all, you all could be arrested." I lectured like an academic who spent his whole life writing papers and books which had hardly any relevance to immediate reality.

She looked at me with disbelief, and she seemed to be confused. Another gentleman came to her stall with four plastic bags, one for fish, one for meat, one for fruits, and one reserved for the vegetables. The bags' elasticity was such that you couldn't easily tear them, and they were so transparent that one could not resist looking at the items they contained. And the fresh blood was dripping from the meat and fish bags. And the men, who carried and dangled the all clear plastics around the shops of the bazaar, took much pride in displaying the meat and fish, to the eyes of the poor average buyers of potatoes and tomatoes.

I took a betel leaf from a nearby stall. I was not in hurry as it was a holiday. My mood got refreshed, and I lazily came to my cycle, and checked again if the eggs were in proper place. I was chewing, and my lips and mouth were red. A fishy smell came from a corner. It was strong, but people didn't mind. They got habituated with this odour. Not all, a few covered nose with sari or kerchief. But most of buyers put fingers on their nostrils for seconds, and then inhaled deeply the smell to restore the pulmonary equilibrium of the air.

"*Bachha* (son), that's why I'm in anxiety. I can't sleep. My head is moving. Pressure and sugar have been high. Oh! My daughter's life is destroyed. I can't imagine how Palash can do such an evil work. He is a good boy. He has no bad habits like smoking, drinking, buying lottery leaf, no *meyer nesha* (lust for women). His friends are all good. How can you do this? Don't think for your wife and child. Couldn't their faces deter you to do such evil deed? What do you lack? Your father is a panchyat, you working well. I gave Shibani gold of Rs. 2 lakhs, khat, bedding, furniture, TV, bike. I also gave Palash's father Rs. 1 lakh hard cash during the night of the marriage. Aeh…you destroy such a golden family! Never think of the face of your child!" She slobbered and sobbed.

Her eyes were wet, and she is wiping them. Her voice was choked. The old woman again offered words of sympathy with a belief in fatality, "Stop crying, sister. What can we do? All's the handiwork of gods. Hari bol, hari bol, hari bol!" She sighed, and began to keenly count the coins. Her eyesight was poor, and she took each coin close to her eyes, checked them, and made separate columns for coins of 1, 2 and 5. She kept not costly vegetables, only some wild shoots, and some common grass and nuts were her precious merchandise.

"All connections are cut between your family and theirs, I think," I observed and waited for her confirmation. And I also guessed the answer, as many such stories of elopement and family tragedy abounded in towns and villages of Bengal. In case of town, the characters were all cultural icons, and the crisis was generally solved either mutual agreements or by the active intervention of the court. It was all hush hush. But in the case of village folks, the story of nuptial calamity spread like the flames of wild forest. And people stopped bathing and eating to relish its sweet savoury juice. They crowded the house of the tragedy, and offered thousands of ways, comments at free.

She spat and coughed, and etched her hands and legs. "Na, beta. Palash is repenting, and he wants to come to my house. My daughter is also willing, and she makes video calls with him thrice a day. Oh...what is it called, oh sending *chobi* (picture) and *maeges* (message) by *mubile* (mobile). I in last month bought a big phone for her at Rs. 15000. I paid Rs. 5000, and the *malik* (owner) of the store is good, and this month I shall have to pay him the rest with no interest. I'm very strict. I said my daughter never to call Palash at my home. I don't want to see his face again. Rascal, idiot! Aeh leaving my *rajkonya* (princess), you are sleeping with a woman of the street. Hai hai beta, what I do? Some days ago a few distant relatives of Palash came to attend a marriage at our neighbourhood. They asked for my daughter's house. Shibani, you know, is a village queen, and everyone pines for her bad luck. Ha, and they came and told us that randi has a nine year girl child. Two years back her husband, a rickshaw puller died, and that *pashani* (devil) ate Palash. Aha ha ha...The boy was so good! He never looked upon any women's face."

I was quite late. The people were hurrying and scurrying. The sounds of hallooing, shouting, bargaining, hawking buzzed the bazaar. Everyone was moving round and round with bags dangling from both hands. I saw some faces for third or fourth times. They couldn't find the items they loved, perhaps. The elderly paced slowly with dry faces and thick spectacles. The young men were all hurried lot, and the jobless youths of picnic parties buying cheap potatoes, and cabbages and hoarded all in big plastic sacks.

"No other member in your family, masi?" I diverted the talk for a change.

"Your uncle is in bed for one year. He can't walk. Lower part of his body is paralysed. My daughter helps him in toiletries, and bathing, and feeding. I can't stop vending. If I stop, we all shall die without food." She said all at a stretch, and I was taken aback by the simplicity of her talks, as if nothing serious happened. There were no tears in her eyes, they were all dried. And her dour face exposed no pains; it was so sober and calm, and quiet. The notes of anxieties and sorrows all were smothered. It seemed she took life as it was.

I said nothing, and looked around. The sun was quite up. I readied the handles of my cycle by exchanging the bags so that balance of weight on both sides could be a bit even.

Masi called me, and asked to come another day to hear the story of her son, aged sixteen only. The boy asked Rs. 30 from her, and she refused, and the boy killed himself by consuming a bottle of pesticides, which she kept hidden in a corner of the room wrapped with paper. And today is the twentieth day of her boy's death!

❖❖❖

4

A SHIRTLESS MAN AT A GRAVEYARD

A late October afternoon in a Murshidabad village.

Kalu dealer died. He fell from the roof and died. Hemorrhage for an hour and untimely death. Villagers of all ages assembled in clean white wear to bury him at Ebadatnagar Burial Ground.

Kalu, aged fifty, partly bald, was a popular man. Black and lean, snub nosed, a patient of high blood pressure and sugar, he suffered a stroke and fell from the roof. His original title was Biswas, Kalu Biswas. But people one day forgot his title and he was hence commonly called as Kalu dealer. Kalu did not mind as he had an authorised ration shop. Sometimes he was pained at the mutilation of his title. Next he was willingly resigned to his fate.

"What will I do with 'Biswas'? Is it going to pay me more? What's wrong with 'dealer'? I have a valid ration shop. Yes, I am a dealer. So people call me dealer," Kalu reasonably argued, and was relieved from the anxiety of pain caused by the mutilation of his ancestors' title. He rather used to wear it as a badge of honour, a marker of his high social status among the poor villagers.

Kalu lay dead on a wooden charpoy at the centre of his yard, fenced with seasonal flowers, some fresh and others dry.

He was ceremoniously bathed and covered with a coffin sheet. Only his face was uncovered. Head is still bandaged, and face was swollen. People of the neighbourhood, their hearts weary and heavy, faces grey and pale, were having a last look at dealer Kalu. They wailed in the name of almighty Allah, and they consoled the bereaved with thousand long drawn words of caress and care. They offered Kalu's wife and son courage and strength to brave the new world. Widow's world! Fatherless world! A cheerless world!

Adjacent to Ebadatnagar Burial Ground there was a primary school. The school had an open green square field. Because of Covid-19 it was closed. The field was empty, and knee high thick *durba* (meadow) grass covered its surface. *Janaja* (funeral) prayer would be held here. So villagers, Kalu's relatives, friends and foes, crowded the ground. The cortege was placed at the centre of the field. Behind the hearse four or five rows of mourners ritually stood for the final prayer for dealer Kalu. Dressed in white, head covered with white skull cap or kerchief the crowd looked like pilgrims destined to a long distant holy land.

The sky was overcast. Accompanied by a mild wind a dark nimbus cloud loomed over the prayer. It suddenly began to drizzle. In ordinary time villagers would have fled and taken shelter under a roof or a shade or even under a tree. But it was a janaja time. Faces were mournful, sad, and solemn with strong religious feelings. Nobody talked. Absolute silence covered the crowd. Noises of running vehicles, coughs and sneezes, clearing throats were though occasionally heard.

Before prayer a customary ritual of asking forgiveness from the crowd for the peace of the soul of dead by Kalu's son and brother was loudly, mournfully made. The mourners instantly forgave him for any loans or dues Kalu owed to anybody or any ill or wound Kalu made to anyone during his life time. The mourners immediately forgave him in consonance.

Amid the drizzle the village maulvi cried for prayer. Rains mingled with tears and sighs and glided through cleanly shaven, bearded cheeks. All were male; boys, young, aged. Women were not allowed to mourn at the cemetery. They were mourning at Kalu's home.

A simple feast by the samaj to which Kalu belonged was made at an open space beside Kalu's house. Two beautiful girls were serving the mourners who had come from far and near. A tarpaulin was cast overhead. Under it plastic chairs and tables were set for the diners. In each table there was a plastic jug for drinking water. Irrespective of the ebb and flow of the wailing the feast continued from late morning to early sunset. Obviously men, women and children were not relishing the tasteless food. They were hurriedly stuffing stomach anyhow, it seemed.

Suddenly a lungi-clad, shirtless, bare headed, lean, patched eyed man, aged under fifty appeared at the burial field from nowhere. He made some round around the crowd. Quite invisible to the mourners he checked and tried to read the contours of every sad face. And he smiled quizzically too. Sometime he looked at the raining sky. Sometime he threw hands to the sky and beat his breast. No one spoke to him. No one looked at him. So he surveyed the faces of the mourners, the coffin, and the trees that fenced the ground and the surroundings. Occasionally he was erratically brushing his head with both hands, killing a mosquito or a fly that pestering his wounded left leg.

The graveyard was wide and dotted with tall bamboo, neem, banana and shimul trees. At base weeds and creepers were fighting for space and the fallen yellow leaves were only witness to this unending violence. In between the school field where janaja prayer was held and the burial ground where the dead would soon be buried there was a chicken farm, fenced with jute sticks. A foul smell filled the farm's air.

Four bearers, Kalu's brother and son and two close neighbours, carried the cortege, and they were assisted by a couple of mourners. The mourning procession was passing haltingly, the bearers were leading from front, and they were silently followed by the sobered crowd. As the earth got slippery they carefully, cautiously, silently entered the grave just dug a while ago. Aroma of fresh soil still lingered in the air.

The rain had just stopped for a while, and streaks of afternoon glow cast an ethereal spell on the burial ground. The grave diggers, the mourners, the trees, the weeds, the sky, the farm – everything looked eerie and quite unnatural.

"Where is the shirtless fellow?" I murmured and my eyes rolled around the grave and the gatherers. The aged, the young, and the children I came across, but nowhere the man I saw. Then I slowed the movement of my eyes, and carefully studied the crowd again. Alas! He was nowhere.

Again the sky went dull. It began to drizzle. The mourners patiently stood in the queue. A few gentlemen unfurled umbrellas, and the rest stood in the rain, wiping foreheads and faces, and they appeared to be fools in the eyes of the umbrella bearers. They were sad, the air was dull and heavy, and the birds forgot to sing. Not even crows cawed or sparrows darted the gloomy sky. No wild flowers swayed either.

I had, however, an advantage. The graveyard, the village, the villagers were unknown to me. So nobody cared, no eyes spread light on me. And surely in my life there would hardly be a chance for my feet to touch the earth of this burial place. So the bonding between me and the graveyard would occupy a permanent niche in my imaginary landscape. In reality I might never visit the graveyard again. This thought made me sad. And soon I found a kind of kindred kinship with the shirtless man. He was invisible to the eyes of the crowd as I was. No mourners asked my name. No mourners asked my whereabouts. Their whispers, sighs, sorrows were whirling around their familial boundary.

Then I saw the shirtless man at a far northern end of the graveyard. He was murmuring and looked sheepish. A fistful of wet leaves he collected and slowly, carefully spreading over a sunken grave covered with weeds and twigs. Now he was brushing his eyes, his head; now he was smiling comically. A couple of bamboo had made an arch over the grave. Rains from the foliages were dripping on it. The man did not care. Drenched he was humming and wailing for the dead buried here. No brick structure or bamboo fence was made around this particular grave. It lay neglected and free and enjoying the freedom of air and earth and the sky.

"Has he lost his mother?" drawing attention of a nearby lanky man I asked.

"Who?" he looked astonished.

"The shirtless man mourning at the corner of the graveyard," I pointed to the corner with my hand.

"Who says this? O, Allah! Who can say this? It's profane, a sin to claim a living woman dead! Allah won't forgive you. *Tauba, tauba*! " the man looked wounded and searched me from head to feet with his small eyes, and he looked confused, and terribly upset.

"What's wrong with him, then?" I plainly put.

"O, evil man, his mother is well, and she is living by binding thousand biris a day. Her eyes are sharp, and hands adept in stitching biris. Her hair is black as tar, and teeth all white as snow. The man is her only child. She has lost her husband when the boy is only two. Snake bite and her man dead. The fatherless boy has day by day grown up to a muscular mason and had gone to Kerala. After two years he had come back home, built a house by the riverside, and married a *sundori* (beautiful) girl, a red rose. Huge feast was thrown and we happily dined and blessed the couple for conjugal bliss. Then one day..." he spat, and brushed his lips with the *gamacha* (napkin) loosely hanging round his long creased neck. His shaven face looked awefully reddish.

"Wait, my turn has come. I don't want to miss chance to pay last tribute to Kalu. During lockdown he helped us. He distributed us whatever he had at his godown – rice, pulse, wheat, suagar, kerosene. He was a good man who always stood by the side of his poor neighbours. We are shocked at his sudden death. But who can violate dictates of Allah!" he haltingly ran towards the mound of Kalu's grave.

I have already paid tribute to Kalu. I was just waiting for my good friend who was unfolding the story of the shirtless man. I looked sideways and saw the people, mournful, sad, and bereft of worldly affairs and daily pursuits. All were thinking of Kalu's fate, and perhaps they were, as maulvi saheb, had just reminded us in his final sermon about our final destination, our grave, *koborer ajab* (punishment at grave). The crowd seemed to have lost zeal in life. Their talks, gestures, movements had suddenly lost earthly connection. They looked thoughtful about their end day. "We all would have to face Kalu's day and our final restroom would be our grave." Such thoughts whirred round the mourners. The trees stood dumb. The birds stopped cooing, and even the winds ceased to blow. Only rains were merciful.

The shirtless man did not move from the corner. He did not pay tribute to Kalu. He was only murmuring and moaning at the northern end. And here the ritual of paying tribute to Kalu by offering fistful of earth over his coffin was going on in tandem. Queue was too long. Some fresh faces are still coming and joining with the mourners for Kalu's last rites.

My good friend, meanwhile, had appeared. His hands were smeared with fresh mud, and he was rubbing hands apparently to make them tidy. He was at peace with himself.

"After the marriage..." I alluded to the thread where he left.

"O, yes, the man was happy with his fragrant rose. And they were peacefully living at the new house he built by the side of the river. His wife was pregnant, oh! I have forgotten to tell you. They were ready to welcome the new member. His mother stitched a couple of *kathas* for the expected baby. She was restless to squeeze the butter skin of the child. In quiet afternoon she would carry the child, taking her to her breast and show her hens, ducks, birds, butterflies, cattle. She would twitch her cheeks, smile at her toothless gums. The man brought fruits and fish from market. He would take care of her pregnant wife. At night he would stroke her swollen belly and the baby wriggled like goldfish in an aquarium. She felt proud and she took utmost care and would routinely follow its movement. If movement was less she looked thoughtful, became apprehensive. Those days were harder." The man removed his skull cap, brushed his face with the end of gamacha, and brushed his muddy slippers against the wet brownish bamboo leaves and began, "Then his wife during delivery died at Berhampore General Hospital.

Doctors could not save the mother either. Mother and the child died. And they were buried at the same grave. The man turned mad, and visited the grave. In earlier days he visited it at each day. Ten years is long time, you know. Time is a great healer. That young man turns now into a dry bone. Still he visits the grave. He does not put earth to anyone's grave. He only reads the faces of the mourners and seeks shelter at his wife's grave where mother and her baby are at eternal sleep." My good friend wiped the corners of his eyes, his voice choked.

"What can be done? All is in Allah's hand. And Allah is most merciful," I sympathized and took his hand.

"From that day he does not wear shirt or anything else on his upper body part," my good friend claimed while smiling like a waning moon, "and with every death his sorrows get resurrected, and he rushes to the corner, and wails for his lost rose and her bud."

❖❖❖

5

A WINTER EVENING

It was a December Sunday evening, foggy, chilly, and bitter. Air was biting hard, and yonder Jaldapara forest, famous for its one-horned rhinos, lay asleep under the quilt of dew. I visited a village, enjoyed daylong the beauty of the forest. Fatigued, in the evening I came back to Galakata haat, adjacent to the forest, drank tea at a crowded shop, made a round around the haat, and surveyed peasant men and women selling and buying grocery, vegetables, fish. Some were burning woods, some smoking, chatting, drinking tea, and abusing the harsh day. Next I waited for an auto to return home at Falakata.

Ten minutes passed. My sweater was soggy with dripping dew. I looked at sides and waited anxiously. Just then an auto jerkily stopped before me. It was almost full.

An Adivasi peasant woman with her half-naked child was stealthily dozing off. Next to her haughtily sat a wealthy, educated lady whose child, bundled with woolen clothes and all, was snoring peacefully at her lap. Auto was running fast, street empty, icy air fiercely kicking and slapping us.

A tiny timorous bulb was dangling overhead. Its light was hazy and could hardly make us visible to one another.

Suddenly at the whisk of a wind the woolen cap slipped a bit out of the child's head. And the panicky rich mother shouted, "Driver, driver, stop."

"What, madam?" warily asked the driver while slowing the speed.

"Stop. My heart will catch cold, her head is bare," she hastily said and began to adjust the beautifully designed cap on her sleeping child.

Auto stopped with a hitch. Passengers, aged men and women, were shaken to the bone, looked red and abused the driver by calling his father's and grandfather's names.

The child's head was fully covered. The rich mother was at ease. She randomly kissed the child, repeatedly examined her darling's socks and gloves, and as an extra protective measure tightly covered her with the red Kashmiri shawl she wore. Satisfied finally she ordered the driver to move.

The sky was dull. Surroundings were foggy. Not a soul on the street was visible. Not a dog was barking or a bird calling or a child crying. It was a gloomy, cheerless evening. The only solace I had was to watch the leaping fires at the yards of the sleepy houses. Peasants sat on their haunches around the fires and baked limbs before retiring to bed.

Again the wind began biting hard. Passengers called the driver to go slow, but he hardly paid ears to his daily passengers. They were uncouth, boorish, lowly weaklings – masons, daily labourers, carpenters, fish sellers, paan sellers, vegetables sellers, plastics sellers, umbrella repair men, wood cutters and the like. It was a regular affair, and he was dead with such complaints, requests, and demands from these poor sops.

Hardly a stop was crossed, the rich woman again shouted and the driver again stopped with a sudden brake. The passengers were thrown out of their seats, and this time they abused the driver with more vehemence. It, however, hardly moved the driver. He was nonchalant. His face was vacant.

"What madam?" asked the driver while painstakingly combing his bald head in the cracked rear mirror.

"I want an extra seat. I'll pay for it. I cannot go home like this. Such poor things! Rotten! " fumed the lady.

"Why, madam? Any problem?" casually he asked.

"I want another seat. I'll pay you," with a reproachful look she asserted.

The driver sensed a trouble. He scratched his head, squinted eyes, and made his mind with the flash of a light. "A rich educated lady! Not *a keu kata* (poor folk)! She must be served. Regulars could be managed. They would howl and growl and be silent soon. But the lady..." cautiously thought the driver. But he feigned.

"Where can I have extra seat, madam? It's packed like an overcrowded boat. Please bear trouble a while. In the next stop all will go down, and it will be empty as a frozen field."

Passengers were annoyed. After the day's gruelling work they were hungry for home. But how could they argue with a sophisticated lady? So they furtively exchanged glances and stayed resigned to their posts.

"Do you offer an extra seat or not? I'll buy it. It's simple. Okay, it'll not work. I'm calling my husband. Do you know my husband? He is a B S F man, posted at Chengrabandah border," warned the irate lady, and she fumbled her lather satchel for her mobile set.

"Madam, please stop. I'll be ruined. I manage. One minute please," pleaded the driver with folded hands. His face was pale, and his legs stirring. Beads of sweat decked his temple. He behaved as if a fire caught him.

"Hey! Filthy fellows, move, keep legs pressed, hands tight....Madam, please," apologetically the driver said. "Hey! Sukhi! Make a room for madam. Move to extreme left," hollered the driver.

Bare footed Sukhi had no woolen clothes, no cotton chadar either. Her child had a running nose, a pale whitish face and dry limbs. She was shivering. Her child like a dead piece of flesh lay pasted to her dry breast.

Sukhi moved to the extreme left without a word. She bore no grudge against the driver. It was a daily affair. She worked in a tea garden, ten miles away from her hut. Her husband was an idle drunker. Last year he died of liver ailment.

"Hey! Old haggard! Move to right end. It's not a private car," blasted the driver to an aged labourer, pouring a packet of gutkha into his wide mouth.

The aged man was sized to the far right. The lady took her extra seat and smiled a victory as if she climbed the Everest.

The auto ran again. The icy wind slapped us fiercely. Sukhi chattered, and her little messy piece of flesh lay cuddled to her breast as a log of dry wood.

❖❖❖

6

AAKHIR

Aakhir, an unemployed youth, aged thirty, tall and slim, dark, is hardworking and sincere. Villagers love him as he helps them both in rain and sun. His mother died a week after his birth, and his father married again. A loveless child!

He had no schooling. Step-mother is cruel and sometime beats him, gives a meager meal a day. Relatives and neighbours shed tears from safe distance, lest he be a burden on them. His father is a nut-seller. From haat to haat, from one fair to another he sells nuts and earns his livelihood. He often stays away from home for a week or two, and when he comes back he behaves in the house like a thief. He never comes out of his yard. His wife abuses him if he talks with his neighbours. So he confines himself within his wife's boundary. And he is happy.

Aakhir, a neglected child thus grows up by flying kites, playing and fighting with friends, catching birds and butterflies, stealing eggs and fruits from neighbourhoods. He is a coarse boy who lacks upbringing. Neighbours abused, complained. But who cares? His father is not at home, and his step-mother is a queen of the village.

Thus grows Aakhir and becomes a youth. Unlike his friends he is industrious, helpful, and illiterate. Many of his friends have joined in army, at various offices in Kolkata. They have wonderful wives and beautiful children. Aakhir does not lose hope. Like Dickens's Mr. Micawber Aakhir believes in his luck – 'something will turn up.' So he passes his days keeping himself cool. Yes, a pall of gloom and despair grips him sometimes. But he sees life around – a farmer is ploughing, a rickshaw puller is sweating, a cobbler is mending shoes, a tailor making clothes, sweepers cleaning streets, garage boys repairing vehicles, birds flying in the sky, flowers blooming at gardens. He regains his strength. Life around him replenishes his blood. And he dreams.

"Aakhir, I have good news for you" hollered his lottery-seller friend, taking him tightly to his breast.

"What?"

"A job, *bondhu* (friend), a job."

"Really? I can't believe my ears!"

"Aakhir, Jhontu is a man of one word. Keru, bring two cups of special tea. Bring a sweet paan. Quick."

"I don't take tea," said Aakhir.

'Keru, two paans. Run my boy, run like a cheetah."

"Ok, boss. Keep a leaf of 1 crore for me," Keru shouted back and ran.

"Take seat, bondhu; feel good, why you are standing like a scarecrow? You have to change your ways. You're uncouth, no manners, no good habits. All these go against the minimum standard and requirement of the job. But you are my childhood friend. A chance falls from the sky! Why do we not catch it?"

Aakhir nods and uncomfortably sits beside Jhontu. A sweet-seller comes, turns the leaves at Jhontu's table, and snatches a bundle and parts.

"Huh...let's come to the point. A position has been vacant. The boy, who works there, suddenly leaves for Delhi. Big city, big people! In Delhi, you know, notes are flying in air at night and day! Anybody can catch! So the boy departs with his girl. Cash and comfort!" lectured Jhontu.

"Where? Is it a garage or a restaurant? " Excitedly Aakhir asked.

"Jhontu is a man of one word, you know. He knows the value of friendship. How can I black or burn your hands?"

"Sorry friend. But I'm illiterate. Who will keep such a useless coin in pocket?" Aakhir asked, his eyes seem to burst in wonder and excitement.

"Don't worry friend. I'm your carrier. Rest your weight on me and feel free," Jhontu heehawed and thumped his back.

Meantime tea is served. Jhontu masticates paan, and spits. As a result words are haltingly coming out his stained thick lips.

"Huh....Allahabad Bank of Mirzapur. Manager is good, kind, full of mercy, a true bhadrolok. Moreover, he is my wife's cousin's brother. He needs an illiterate hand. Salary is not bad – Rs.3000 per month. Sunday is yours. You can enjoy, you can do what you like," earnestly pursued Jhontu.

"But....Mirzapur is long distance," Aakhir feebly said and worriedly scratched his head.

"You have a cycle, and I don't think 20 kms up down is a bump to your future smooth street. Don't you know many of my friends cover 200 kms a day for a paltry sum? No, no, no. I don't expect such an excuse from you," Jhontu rued and he looked disappointed.

"Bondhu, I'm sorry. I know I hurt you. Don't be at cross with me," Aakhir pleaded and ordered tea.

"Bondhu, today a job is a life, and for it people are selling their huts, fields, cattle and even utensils. But I'm not asking for such an extreme step. I know you have no land or cattle. Your stepmother is a fat pig. Your father is dead," Jhontu continued.

"Who say it? My father is not dead," protested Aakhir.

"But does he take care of you? Does he love you?"

"No. He is selling nuts in fairs round the year. He has no time. Moreover, my stepmother keeps him in chains when he is at home."

"So, he's dead. That is my point."

Aakhir sat silent with his drooping head between his hands. Minutes passed. The sun began to wane spreading a glow over the village.

"Aakhir, you are my close friend. How can I ask a bribe? But you know even a dead man opens mouth at its scent."

"How much?"

"You are my childhood friend. We have grown up playing and dining together. How can I demand? Think what makes you please," softly Jhontu said.

So at the cost of first month's salary Aakhir got the job of a sweeper in Allahabad Bank of Mirzapur. He goes early in the morning and comes home late in the evening. Four floors, four toilets, he daily cleans. Manager is happy with his new recruitment. No ads, no interview. But such a good hand! He never crosses, never complains, and never asks for a leave. Ah! What a heavenly hand!

This way seven years passed.

Aakhir, meantime, married a girl of his choice and had a child. With his meager salary he can hardly manage his family's burden. So one day his wife advises him to ask the manager, a gentle man, for a pay hike.

"Seven years and not a sigle coin added! You are a fool; manager is cheating you. He is sucking your blood! It's plain. You are too dull," his wife chided.

Next morning Aakhir bore his wife's word, bruised, gathered courage, and finally made his mind.

"May I come in, sir?"

"Come in, please" the manager dryly said without raising his head from a heap of files.

"Sir,"

"Ooh! Where is the loan file of Bony Blouse Enterprise? 2 crore project! Party will arrive soon. What a calamity! Ooh!" The manager muttered and he looked worried.

"Sir, if you add some extra rupees, whatever you like, from the coming month I can save my family," timidly asked Aakhir. His eyes were teary, and voice choked. "I never asked for extra single paise for seven years. Sir, but I am not single now…I have a family, wife child…how I can I mange home? …Sir, market is fiery, you know all, and you are my father. You are my mother. Please add some extra and save my family…."

"From tomorrow, Aakhir, you're free. I have a long list of waiting candidates. I can buy them at lower rate anytime. Way up and down, they are pestering me. Many of their fathers and mothers are my friends. But, you're doing fine, that's why I keep you. It's palin and simple. Keep your emotion at home. It's an office. Rules and regulations of RBI I must obey. My hands are tied. I have been waiting for the day, and it has come in the end! Gods are merciful! Why do you still stand like a useless old ass? Have I not told you, my boy, you are now free! Find another place. Find another father. The world is too big! Best of luck! Have a zing time ahed! Still standing like a beggar? Will you go my boy or shall I call my gurads?"

❖❖❖

7

AN AAYA IN TRAP OF CORONA

A 2020 March morning at a Clerk's house in a suburban town in West Bengal.

The world is shaken with the spread of deadly, highly contagious corona virus. Over one lakh fifty thousand people of different nationalities are reported to have been infected across the globe, and thousands have died in its wake. Countries have shut down malls, multiplexes, public gatherings. Checks, screenings, and quarantine facilities are being installed at airports, ports, borderlines. Citizens are warned travelling to foreign countries. Schools, colleges, offices across the country are partially closed for a fortnight. Business houses order their workers to work from home. Religious places are also closed.

People are scary. They prefer to be confined within four walls. Streets are deserted. Trains, buses run irregularly. The town is cheerless. Parks, tea shops and restaurants are closed.

The office of the Clerk is closed for a fortnight. The Clerk, aged around fifty, short, well-built, workaholic, has an abrupt and unexpected holiday for half a month. He stays at home and works from home.

The lady of the house is a school mistress. They keep an aaya for their toddler Prince.

"Rumi, don't put your bag on balcony. Take paper and wrap it up, and keep it on the high stool," orders the Mistress while warily unlocking the door.

The Clerk, sitting on sofa, is flipping day's paper. He looks worried. One has died in City Hospital. He had returned from Arab and was suffering from fever, cold, and coughs for a week.

"Is the bus crowded, Rumi?" asks the Clerk.

"No, dada it is empty as a crematory. First time in my life I get a seat by the window," Rumi joyously confirms.

The Clerk and his wife look relieved. They think of dismissing Rumi for days. But she is a widow, has a school-going daughter at home. Her husband had fled with an aged woman a year ago. Her life depends on her work. Moreover she is good – punctual, knows when to talk and when to keep lips shut, regular, takes prior permission for a leave and dances, sings all day with Prince. A good aaya is a lottery. Many were hired and freed – quarrelsome, irregular, irresponsible, dirty, and diseased. But Rumi is freed from all. So they are suffering from indecision.

"Rumi, change and take a hot bath," Mistress advises staring at her.

"Why? At dawn I have just shampooed in a pond?"

"Pond?" Mistress is taken aback. And the Clerk jerks up from the sofa.

"Our tubewell is not working for a week, Madam," plainly Rumi put. "But you know without a bath I don't leave home," Rumi boasts.

"Do you know the gizzard-tap?"

"No, Madam."

"Right one. Discard your used soap. Take this new one," Madam Offers a lifebuoy soap case and returns back to her husband.

Sounds of splashing and pouring water, coughing and sneezing are heard in the bathroom.

"Free her for a fortnight," Madam anxiously put. I am scared.

"But..."

"No ifs and buts. Money we sacrifice. Prince is our only future. His safety we seek first," Madam exhorts. "Don't you know they are too low, living in diseased ghettos and slums, have no sense of hygiene. Give her...Oh! Let's calculate. Fifteen days into two hundred...three thousand. Pay and dismiss her. I feel ill, honey."

"Money is not falling from the sky, honey! Not a paise government gives me extra," the Clerk defends. His face is tight. He looks vexed. His body is stiff.

"What can we do? After a long harrowing times we fortunately have Rumi. If she leaves, we have to shed tears again. A good aaya is a lottery today! Without Rumi we cannot sail. Your boss will chide you and my headmistress will wear a glum face. Fed or unfed I hate a sullen face. It's so irritating! Disgusting!" Mistress goes to bed room, lifts a side of the net, and carefully covers Prince with a light cotton *chadar* and checks and plant kisses on his forehead.

Rumi comes out of the bathroom. Mistress checks if the toiletries, buckets, mugs are in place. Everything is in disarray. Germs spread! Germs everywhere! She is shocked and shaken.

"Have you used my Lotus face wash?" angrily Madam asks.

"Why do I so? I carry my face wash in my pouch," she retorts and takes a small bottle of violet liquid out of her dusty bag.

"Go straight to basin, and wash both hands with hand wash," Madam shouts.

"Rumi, Keep it and take rest for two weeks. Don't visit fairs and friends. Don't visit melas and *khelas* (sports). Repair your tubewell first. Don't take bath in pond. Take care of Munni. Cook food and eat within walls," the Clerk gives her a bundle of clean notes.

"Babu, I cannot take advance. I sweat and I claim," Rumi says and takes only two notes and returns the bundle. "Call me when you need. And meantime if any home I get, I will serve for now. *'Babu apnara boddo valo aachen...apnara dakle na kemon kore bolbo'* (Babu, you are too good...if you call, how can I say 'no.'"

❖❖❖

8

AT A BARBER'S SHOP

"Rents due for seven months? My wife abuses me at each dead of night. Pay or leave. No more words I want to hear. It's simple as palin water." The barber looked bitter and helpless.

The lanky boy in tattered jeans and worn out slippers put a nonchalant face. His teeth and tongue are deep marooned, his thick hair neatly cut and carefully parted in the middle.

"Have a seat, sir," the barber-boy asked me with a forced smile on his square face.

The boy was chewing paan masala, and now and then stealthily glanced at me. Meantime his carpenter friends came hallooing and the boy left the shop for day's work.

"Sir, bad boy, very bad! Staying at my home for a year. Whatever he earned, he squandered on liquor with friends in the evening, and he came home in empty hand," mourned the barber.

"How do you know?" I asked bluntly.

"Will I shave you?"

"Do I need? It's one day's growth."

"No, you'll look smart. Moreover your beard grew all white. Shave it, sir. Is the wedding party tomorrow or tonight?"

"Hey! Who is wedding whom?"

"How can I say? I think so. People nowadays prefer shaving at home. And on important occasions like marriage or death do they come at my shop."

"Who's the boy?"

"Oh! He is a carpenter. He is quite good at work. Sir, what I tell? Very bad, a shameless fellow! A rotten scoundrel!"

The shop is bare. The mirror is rusted. One leg of the table is supported on a pile of broken bricks. When you sit, it gives a sudden jerk. The tin shade was painted ages ago. And the lather tubes are almost dry scattered in utter disarray and covered with dust. And the lemonade bottle lies uncorked. The barber, aged fifty or so, has a snub nose, and a stale face and teeth milk white, eyes big and red.

He lathered me harshly. I felt pain, but kept my ease. He then went to buy a packet of blades. I sat and looked at the mirror and immediately turned my eyes away in fear!

He gasped, and his heavy breath fell on me. "Don't mind, sir. I make you wait. I'm really sorry," said he while shaving and putting the lather into a tin glass.

"Not at all, I rather enjoy your smooth hand. And by the way you call the boy bad! Why? What's wrong with him? He looks such a nice boy!"

"He is a man of two children! He looks so, sir," the barber sneered and continued frenziedly, "we give him a room on rent. And for a year not a paise he has paid. Every day my wife shouts him to leave...but the pale face of his poor wife and two smiling children at her lap steal us. No food at home, the children eat and sleep with us. No fault of Rita. She regularly fights with her drunkard man at day's end when he returns home in empty hand. How long does she bear? Each night he brawls and beats her, and she cries and cries and in the end takes shelter under my roof."

The barber thrashed me from head to toe with a dirty napkin and drew his mouth close to my ear and confided, "Sir, the man has more qualities. All I can't share. But if you give words I can tell you the most amazing one."

"Phoo! Why do I tell? I've no time to meddle with that. I swear."

The barber was assured and whispered, "He sleeps with his mother-in-law. Such a bad guy he is. And you say he's a nice boy! Ugh…"

"How do you know?" I feigned not to be surprised.

"He told me so. My ears got red, sir, when I learnt it first time. And I pleaded him not to share the secret with anybody else," the barber spat in disgust.

"But he looks such a nice boy. Eyes deep and dark, broad brow, a faint smile gleaming on his thin lips. A very likeable boy! Such a nice face!"

"Sir, don't mind. Can I ask a question?" the barber plainly put.

"Go ahead. I always welcome question. Questions keep me alive."

"What's your age, sir?"

"Is it a question? Look at my skin and you get the clue. Moreover, people say age is just a number. So what you do with my age?" smilingly I put.

A young mother entered with her child. His hair was to be cut. The boy was crying bitterly. He would not cut hair. He would buy a racquet. He would buy balloons.

Young mother sat on the bench. She unlocked her mobile set and gave it to the child. The boy immediately stopped crying and nagging. His tender fingers were scratching the screen, his eyes glued to the You Tube cartoons and mother got instant relief. She cheerfully waited for her turn.

"Sir, you are highly educated, experienced. I am eight pass. You are a ship of knowledge. But I don't believe what you believe. Face is merely mask we wear. Face betrays."

I soon fell in love with the barber and since the day I began to frequent his shop off and on.

❖❖❖

9

BALOO

"A worthless wishy-washy fellow! No work, no family!" muttered the old man, and sat silently beside Baloo under the shade in the mango grove, wearing a reproachful look.

Baloo's mother died when he was two, and his father fled with a girl of the neighbourhood almost a decade ago. He had no friends, no relations. He grew up working at villagers' homes, fields, herding their cattle, rearing their chickens, hens, roosters. Days of hardships were gone. He lived in his lonely hut fenced with betel nut trees, and he kept some goats and pigeons and bees.

He no longer worked in the fields. But when he was sought by some landed peasants, he helped them. And he took no wages. Instead, a measly meal, a pouch of tobacco, and a pot of *haria* (deshi liquor) were his usual call.

And the day when Baloo went to sow or harvest, his hut was empty, desolate. The birds forgot their mounting, the goats baaing, and bees ceased buzzing. And when he returned in the evening the birds perched on him, lovingly scratched him from head to toe, and cooed. And the goats began bleating louder and louder, and the bees buzzed again.

"Baloo, you are a happy chap! I envy you!" said the old peasant with ire in his voice.

Ballo took a sidelong glance at the doleful face of the old peasant, and claimed, "Why not? I've the key to happiness."

"What's it?" bluntly the old man queried.

"It's as easy as an old shoe," quipped Baloo.

"Say if you like. I'm an aged man, and I don't like riddle at this age," woundedly he said.

"Why are you so restless? A hasty man can't be in cloud nine in life or death!"

The old man didn't speak. And Baloo eyed the luxurious chiaroscuro on the dead leafy bed where they both sat for a fleeting relief from the fiery sun.

"Are you a sage?" asked the old man with a sneer.

"Much wiser than a sage or a seer, man!" claimed Baloo, and he continued, "hear, shun man, and love the trees, the hills, the skies, the birds and the beasts, and be happy. It's so simple. But you worship gold, and it steals the beauty of your life. You hoard and one day will die! You steal the toil of children and women. You kill beasts and birds. So bliss eludes you!"

Baloo spat, and lit a bidi. His eyes shone bright, and face was flushed.

Silence followed for a while. And then Ballo resumed, "You keep the calves half-fed, unfed, and inject their mothers to fill your pails twice a day. You are a blood sucking leech found in plenty in our forests!"

Silence followed again. The old man wore a quizzical face. Then suddenly he broke into a wild rage. He glared at Baloo and yelled, "I'm not a bird-keeper, and never want to be. Gold I need, and with it honour comes. My family was poor, and in most of the days we went to bed unfed. Brothers were lazy, and they gambled. Father was ill, and mother worked at Chowdhury house as a domestic hand. One day I left home, and slaved at sweet shops, tea shops, saw mills, fields, forests. Fifty years thus I passed. Then I bought some acres of lands, and built a house. If I didn't chore in strangers' shops and homes, if I didn't kill trees and beasts, what would happen to me? A poor boy would die poor!" His eyes were fiery.

Beyond the mango grove the sun was merciless. Ponds were parched, and fields cracked into million pieces.

The old peasant continued, "Baloo, I hate birds, bees, butterflies, trees. What I do with that!? It won't make me rich. When I see a bird, I weigh its flesh."

"You're a leech I know, but a howling fox…Uh…?"

"And you a paltry pigeon keeper?" the old man argued.

"You're blind to life's haloed paths, man! Born a dog and die a dog! Phoo!" Baloo loudly spat in disgust.

"Haloed paths! Who walks there?"

"One who worships the nature – the large liquid sun, the ecstatic noon, the rhapsodic twilight, the sparkling night, the silver moon, the singing hills, the rustling trees, the moaning forest, the sea blue sky dotted with languid cloudlets, chattering birds, and the green fields, and the wild lianas coiled on tall, tall trees."

"Ugh! …the things you say are at my arm's distance. I find no bliss in them. They are natural, and so mundane. The sun will rise and die every day. What will I do with that? Does it fill my belly?" The old man smoked, and put on a sour face.

"Stop talking of belly…," Baloo roared in rage.

The old peasant gaped. He muttered, and made a search for the birds among the leaves.

"I find no birds in the branches."

"Is it so? There are no birds in the branches."

The old man was at a loss. In old days he hunted in the forests. In monsoon when the rain didn't cease for days and weeks they would go to the forest, and cut trees, and cleared miles after miles at sepulchral nights. Such a dreadful life he had led and Ballo battered him with his haloed paths of goats and gnats, birds and bees! His head whirled. He heaved a heavy sigh.

Baloo, meantime, hummed for his girl who in a nearby village made a home with a droughty woodman, and had two lovely children.

❖❖❖

10

A BURNING PYRE

The scene was magnificent. A pyre was burning and the peasants, all drunk, were chanting *bolo hari, hari bol; bolo hari, hari bol.* Some were crying loud, some were sobbing, some sat terribly silent as stone.

It was monsoon. The fields and ponds were alike with water everywhere. The rain stopped for a while and the dark clouds disappeared. Instead, streaks of fleecy cloudlets covered the face of the setting sun. A huge tamarind tree stood resolute by the burning pyre.

The pyre was laid on a rugged brick structure in a raised land by the side of a big pond. Men and women sat on haunches circling it. A thick column of grey smoke billowed upwards. Now and then, the peasants sprinkled kerosene onto it, and the fire flashed and dazzled the mourners' eyes.

The boy was half-burnt; his skull and bones were not engulfed yet. Men, meantime, stopped mourning, and women, eyes swollen and faces weary and pale, were sobbing still.

"Ahaha! Such a nice boy he was!" mourned a middle aged fat peasant woman.

"He never looks at our girls. He walks fixing his eyes to the ground. He has no foul habits like drinking, smoking or gambling. Ah! Such a nice boy he was," rued another peasant woman.

"A model lad he was. Tomorrow he would be betrothed and tonight he died. Ahahaha! So early the boy took his life! A girl might have a past. And for that he died!" grieved the fat woman and spat with a reproachful face.

"Don't call her a girl. She's a *randi* (prostitute). Ahaha! The *daini* (witch) ate the boy up before laying her step into her love's nest," protested a good looking housewife with large liquid eyes and floating dark hair.

The fat woman nodded and said, "Huh…I heard her story. Her mother eloped with a man, and her father drank at Jharia's shop. Day long he sat there and drank. At night he came back and beat her. She didn't resist. She bowed at his feet and lay cold like a lump of dead flesh, and her father out of rage beat her more. Then he howled, groaned, and spasmodically kissed her wounds. Villagers knew it all. They were habituated to evening scene. And they didn't meddle. The same story played at day after day."

"The girl then became desperate," the fat woman continued. "She began to play truant from school and visited the line hotels. Thus she earned a few sullied notes and with it she took care of her ailing father."

The pyre was smouldering. Women chattered and chattered now in animation, now in hush hush. And men were drinking and brawling at a farthest corner. It seemed they had already forgotten the suicide of the lad.

The fat woman raised her hawkish voice and asked, "Arre, tell me, who die for a girl? Stupid boy! Is there any lack of girls? So many beautiful butterfly girls were fluttering around. My own sister remains at home unmarried for seven years. What's bad about the match?"

None disagreed and many of them even claimed that it would have been a *manik joar* (a perfect match) as the boy had no voice and your sister no ears.

Meantime the sun secretly sank, but the rumours didn't die. It was a life time chance. Usually the rustic housewives kept them shut to their crooked huts at day. And in the evening they sat on the front yards and gossiped. The topic was invariably dull, old, and cold. But today is a funeral day! And the bride was a harlot!

For an hour and a half the pyre was smouldering, and heavy smelly smoke wrapped them all. Some spat, some coughed, and some sneezed. The body lay hidden under a huge stack of logs. The drunkards now sprinkled kerosene, now led bamboo poles underneath it. Each time the knots of the poles burst, the peasants jostled in joy, and shouted *bolo hari*. A few hurriedly brought a pair of worn-out tyres, poured kerosene on them again, and threw them under the pyre. The fire leaped head high and the entire place was alight. The women who were still busy with slanders took sudden notice of the rising flames. They gave a mournful look at the angry fire and sighed for the boy.

The boy was burning and his parents were wailing. They sat on a heap of broken musty bricks, frenziedly tossed their heads and thumped breasts with sickening hands. Neighbours clasped them. A woman took a pail of slimy water, and poured on their heads. Another took a hand fan and began to air the bereved parents.

Nobody noticed the arrival of the night. The fire ate the boy up. The women trudged towards their huts. The father sat, laying one hand on his shriveled, freckled face, and the boy's mother, pale, hair disheveled, sat beside him petrified. Her eyes seemed to be popped out. Nobody could read their faces, such a funny look they wore!

Darkness thickened. The crowd thinned. The dying sparks twinkled amid the debris of ashes. The sky was overcast again, and a fine drizzle set in. Some peasants ran for a shelter in a nearby tin shade. The parents didn't move. Crystal drops of rain trickled down their wrinkled cheeks. Four or five drunkards, drenched in the drizzle, took a mango twig each. They queued, and one by one put a twig on the dying pyre.

An hour passed. The drizzle ceased, and from the gloomy sky stars began to twinkle. A cold breeze blew. The peasants felt cold. Minutes ago four drunkards hauled boy's parents to home.

The boy was burnt, and the peasants in the end crushed his skull with bamboo poles.

The drunkards now plunged into the nearby pond and they began to admire themselves in the rippling waves. They soaped and gurgled. The yellow frogs croaked and the crickets ceaselessly sang. Yonder the fireflies waved up and down over a thickened bush. No night birds hoot. Foxes squeaked in the distant bamboo bush, and somewhere in the village the dogs whined.

The peasants gave a last look at the dead pyre and dragged themselves to their neighbourhood hoarsely chanting *bolo hari, hari bol*. The half-asleep children got scared at bed and clutched at their mothers. The old and the dying counted their waning days, and felt sad for Dahia. Such a nice boy he was! Such an ill luck he met in end!

❖❖❖

11

DUKHI

There was a rickety paan shop at a few steps away from the mouth of the station D. Dukhi, a lean, wizened man, aged over sixty, owned it. He was singular in that among a half dozen surrounding shops he alone sold paan. While others dealt in cosmetics, stationary items, fruits, beverages, biri and cigarettes, snacks and tea and sweets, Dukhi was happy with a bundle of betel leaves, two tiny jars of betel nuts, a plastic pot of cardamoms, a stack of empty cigarette cases, and a squat pot of lime with a spoon half-hidden into it.

His tiny tarpaulin-covered shack was shy and almost invisible. On his left side stood a crowded tea shop. On right hand stood a stationary shop. There were benches, chairs and stools before the shops. It was a clean and open space. Passengers, exhausted with day's dealings, detrained, drank, smoked, and gossiped, got refreshed here. There was a kadam tree beside Dukhi's shop. A cluster of crows were shrilly cawing on its boughs. A madman was chasing a hairless dog at a distance.

Hot summer afternoon. The sun was hidden behind the blocks but its crimson glow added an aura to Dukhi's shop and its surroundings.

A young gentleman, tall, fair, well-dressed, with two trolleys in hands, stopped by the side of Dukhi's shop, and he asked for a cup of tea from a nearby stall. He thoughtfully sipped while wiping beads of sweat from his face and looked around for a smoke. His eyes suddenly fell on cigarette cases stacked at Dukhi's sleepy shop. A glow crossed his flushed face.

"A navy cut, king size" the young man casually threw a twenty rupee note.

"It's not a cigarette shop, sir," excused Dukhi with a queer laugh, an expression of benign grace and gratitude. He looked a bit funny in the dying light of the sun.

"Cases stacked in plenty, and you deny me one!" the young man was confused and put on an angry face.

"Empty, sir," politely Dukhi said, clearing his throat, and added, "you are not alone. People often mistake me, put on angry face, hurl hot words, but I don't mind."

"What's their use, man? Discard them into a bin. Why do you keep those empty cases?" the young man blasted and squinted eyes.

A gust of hot wind blew and dry, brown kadam leaves rained on Dukhi's shredded shack. The tin shade, covered with a thick layer of dry kadam leaves, looked splendid, as if freshly painted.

"It's a long story, sir," sighed Dukhi, and he at once changed the topic, "where are staying, sir?"

"Why? It's my home town," quipped the gentleman.

"I think you are a stranger and come here for some business or official tour. Sorry sir. Old age has its follies! Eyes fail too!" Dukhi coughed.

"Have you no children? It's time for you to stay at home and enjoy your residual days with ease and grease," the gentleman was softened by the open nature of Dukhi, and he took pity on Dukhi.

"No," drily the old man said while making a paan for a regular man waiting patiently by the side of the shop and closely following their talks as if he was a spy.

"Hey! Grey-haired haggard! Tomorrow you'll go to grave, and you are still cheating! Befooling strangers! Sir, he has two fine sons. One works in municipal office, another teaches in a school," boomed Babloo, a building contractor, pot-bellied, bald, dwarf, middle aged man with paan-stained thick lips, and bloodshot eyes.

"Babloo, who calls you to ladle my *dal* (a split grain)? Go out of my sight. Never come again to my sides!" barked the old man like a mad dog. And he carelessly wrapped the paan with a piece of paper and flung it at a safe corner of his shop. He was visibly perturbed and angry.

Dukhi then shouted a lanky boy and ordered him to bring a cigarette.

The gentleman waited patiently. He was not in hurry. His parents had died two years back. He was an I T professional and now established in Bengaluru. Once a year he used to visit his home town. Old friends had faded. Ancestral home had been a safe nest for pigeons and spiders. The flower garden had gone dry. He had come to sell the house. Once or twice he thought of selling it. But later he changed his mind. Now a rich party showed interest, and he was firm in his decision of disposing it off.

"Sir, take it, please" happily Dukhi handed over him the cigarette.

The young man was startled and scared. He was lost in wayward thoughts. His mind was wavering. His childhood, his school days, days of afternoon boating with his parents in the river B, his parents' last lonely days and their cremations at the bank of river B – heavily settled on him. He looked cowered, lifeless, and sad.

"Yea, oh," he tried to wear his poise. He took it, sloppily lit and began to soberly smoke.

A while later Dukhi's rage subsided. He then unburdened himself thus.

"Sir, Babloo is true. We have two able sons. But they have been gobbled up by their in-laws. With money and ease they have bought my sons. And they now fear to tread our yard. We are poor. With sweat and blood we have nursed them. Now they live in flats in town's posh area. And we (he points to an old veiled woman who is droopingly watering the front of the shop as a preparation for evening prayer) in illness and woes are destined to fend for ourselves. Are they our sons? We have no sons, sir!" Dukhi lamented at a stretch and gasped for breath, and his wife chided him.

"If anything happens this time, I'll not take you to hospital. I warn you again and again not to talk of them to anybody. But who hears whom? Our sons are happy. Let them stay happy, babu." The old lady began to wipe her moist eyes with the end of her sari.

The young man was embarrassed. Dukhi, however, did not pay heed to his wife's warning. He resumed.

"Sir, once I used to sell cigarettes of all brands. My stall was a household name among the city smokers. From this stall we managed our rice and dal, and bore the cost of children's education too. Now they are established and we don't need much money. We are two sickly souls. So why do I sell harmful tobacco at this age? I keep these empty cases in fond memory of our children who in our golden days climbed my shoulders, scratched my back, and pestered their mother for balloons, trophies, toys. We see the cases and feel the pulses of our children." Tears welled up in the corners of the eyes of the aged parents.

The gentleman fell ill at ease. He was doubly saddened. He wanted to go home. He wanted to be freed from the fetters of the poor and the impoverished. He wanted to forcibly erase the stains of his childhood days of this city. He settled to begin afresh.

The sun was slowly sinking. Crows on the kadam tree were now carousing fiercely. Soon they would fell asleep.

"Uncle, getting late. Meet you again another day," hurriedly said the young man.

"*Accha baba*," Dukhi instantly nodded and called a known rickshaw puller.

Both of them knew that they would perhaps never meet again.

And the young man waved Dukhi while departing.

Dukhi waved him back, and next began to languidly make a paan for a regular like Babloo.

❖❖❖

12

THE HEADMASTER OF FATEHPUR

A cloudless March afternoon in Berhampore, a suburban town in West Bengal.

"Let's have tea, Sir," I hinted.

As usual the retired headmaster did not welcome my move.

"It's not my home," I smiled and argued.

"So what? I don't take tea at home or outside," reiterated the headmaster, a half-bald, snub-nosed, well-built, medium height man.

He is my daughter's tutor. He is a man of science, does not believe in astrology or apparition. I like his coming and going. Silently he comes and silently he takes leave. Never asks money for the month. He is sullen. And if he smiles, it is dry as bone.

The headmaster is a surprise. I meet him towards the dull days of his life. He has perhaps shared his days of gold and honey with someone somewhere, I think. His resigned look is an onslaught on my inquisitive psyche. I fail to strike a meaningful conversation with him. It pains me. Whenever I offer him tea for talk, he douses my fire, "Another day." And that day has never come.

Today I get an opportunity. He has come for releasing a book on Syed Badrudduja at Grant Hall. When the ceremony is over, I drag him to Benuda's tea shop, located just at the opposite of Grant Hall. The teashop is an oasis among unending rows of dry, dreary blocks. Painters, poets, writers, documentary makers, sculptors, singers, cover designers anytime you'll find there. You'll also find shoemakers, fruit sellers, hawkers, shopkeepers, sales girls, sales boys, beggars. Elections are round the corner. So the party flag bearers, poster boys, wall writers mark their absence.

Benuda's teashop is also known for its smell and dust. I dusted off a chair and made headmaster cozily sit on it. The afternoon was hot and humid. An old ceiling fan with huge scarred blades was tiredly screeching overhead.

Headmaster would not drink tea but when I repeatedly requested, he could not avoid. He sipped a cup of sugarless liquor tea. It seemed he was taking a bitter liquid. Such was the expression he put on his otherwise ruddy face.

"I know why you call me," he pointed out suddenly, "and that's why I am hesitating."

I fell from the sky. I had no money with me. And he was hinting his last month's due. He never asked his due. But today when I have no money in my wallet and he...

"How are you going, Sir? You look tensed!" I diverted the track for my rescue.

He did not speak. He only sighed. I never asked about his family or home. It would be an encroachment on my part I always thought. Moreover, timely he comes, teaches and departs. Never have we got the chance for a leisurely talk.

Initially he used to send me wishes such as good morning, have a nice day, or a bucket of paperless roses too via messenger. He also sent me heart-healing messages on especial days, festival days. But I was not sincere in feedback. So oneday he stopped.

From one of my friends I came to know that he has a house, his wife is a health worker and he has two sons. Nothing more. 'But why is he so sullen? What ails the man?' I thought thousand times. But I am still clueless.

"Siddik saheb, I'm getting weak. Not physically. I have no sugar or pressure. Eyesight too is perfect. I can read paper without glasses. At every night I drink a litre of milk even at this age. It keeps me going through the rugged terrain of life.

"Rugged terrain! You have a home of your own, your wife is earning still. You have no daughter to be married off, only two sons. They will find their ways." I said nonchalantly.

"You live in a fool's paradise!" he rued, "I've blocked their ways." Headmaster looked ashen. Beads of sweat dappled on his face and forehead.

"How? Being a dutiful father you can't," I gaped.

A silence followed. He looked at sideways. Nobody was following us. He looked a bit comfortable.

"It's family matter," he began, "how can I share it? Yes, we have no daughter. And our sons have grown up. I am not worried about Rakesh, my elder son who changes one company and finds another in every month. He is clever, hardworking and practical. What he gets at month's end is enough to run a family. So he is not our concern."

"Happy to hear, sir. What's about the younger one?" I casually asked.

"Water, my tongue is dry," headmaster asked.

Benuda gave him a bottle and smiled at us. He admires unknown faces. But to headmaster it is a strange place surrounded by strange people.

He was the headmaster of Fatehpur High School for thirty years. School was his second home. Hardly had he taken a leave in his long service life. To him work was worship. Playing football and badminton, gardening, organizing quiz, debate and extempore, creating scientific temperament among students were some of his old hobbies. Updating Service Book of his staff, maintaining their Provident Fund, updating midday meal distribution records, etc. – all he did at home singlehandedly by burning midnight oil. For thirty years no staff had the ability to raise a finger at him or his work. He was a neat and clean man. and he was proud of his clean dealings.

Did he not believe his colleagues? He did. But he did not like their lackadaisical attitude. Work must be finished before the scheduled date. It was his work-ethics. So he brought home his colleagues' service books, ledger books, etc. His wife did not like it. But ultimately she resigned and left her husband to his fate. Thus he hardly found time for caring his children. His wife too brought them up a bit indulgently.

"Did he get Shiksha Ratna?" You might ask.

"No, he did not. To have the award a teacher besides her/ his academic brilliance, administrative skill, needs extra qualities which he miserably lacked."

"So sad! Good people have no value in today's market-driven society!" You might mourn.

I did not agree. They are invaluable asset for the health and well being of our society.

Headmaster gulped water, wiped forehead with a kerchief and said, "Ritish is a lover. He is jobless. He writes poetry and loves a girl, Pritha, a WBCS aspirant and she has qualified the main. Will Pritha marry my boy? Never! We fail to convince him the reality. A jobless poet! Ha ha ha! Today I give him two hundred for her ice cream; tomorrow his mother will give him five hundred for her facial foam. We have been doing this since 2015. Love makes him lonely. He has no friends. His room is his world. The walls are covered with Pritha's photos. Laila Majnu kind of love! He will not live without Pritha, but she will not now marry my boy. Bankers, businessmen, engineers, lawyers, and professors are honking cars round the clock around her house."

"Your boy is an emotional fool!" I bluntly put.

"Poets are fools and Plato is, thus, right in banishing them from his ideal Republic." He nodded.

"But you are not Plato!"

"Yes, I am a headmaster of Fatehpur," sadly he laughed, "I don't believe in a loveless world ruled by only artificial intelligence, dry logic, money, profit, figures and facts, digits and diagrams, greed and selfishness. I've spent my whole life for the cause of selfless love. I've spread light in darkness. I love my boys and girls – first learners from poor, peasant backgrounds. I have watered the seedlings and they have sprouted forth new leaves and borne flowers and fruits. Many of them are now established in four corners of the world. When I meet them my heart leaps in the sky. No, not because they earn huge money but they are good human beings. Compassionate, grateful, they truly value love, honour and sacrifice. I have no regrets in life."

The headmaster beamed, his eyes shone. He looked somewhat relieved from the pains that always beat at his bones.

Benuda while ladling tea pan suddenly opened a fresh page of his old diary. He handed over it to him, "Name and mobile no, sir."

Headmaster hesitated, looked at me, and slowly wrote his name and no and took leave.

"See! A few men still walk on earth," Benuda philosophized.

I said nothing. My eyes were on Benuda's dusty, cobwebbed shelves packed with old books, old diaries, old mementos, crumpled yellow papers, and empty cigarette cases.

❖❖❖

13

IN MEMORY OF BHASHA SHAHID ABUL BARKAT

By a dusty roadside a tarpaulin covered shack was littered with over hundred stone slabs of varying sizes and shapes. A man, aged around sixty, lean and tall, thick spectacled, was engraving a rectangular piece of black granite. From head to toe he was coated with dust and flecks of the stone. The slab was to be etched in memory of a legendary name, a bhasha shahid, Abul Barkat who along with Salam, Rafiq, Jabbar, Shafiur and many others sacrificed their life on February 21, 1952 in Dhaka for the sake of their mother tongue Bangla.

Madhu, the owner, aged between forty and fifty, short and bald, bulging bellied, blood-shot eyes, paan stained lips, was smoking, sitting on his worn out stool. He was muttering and thoughtfully surveying his empire of stone slabs.

"Lal, what're you up to still?" asked Madhu in a racy voice.

"Babu, I'm giving a finishing touch to the name plate ordered by the Headmaster of Hekmat High School. He repeatedly warns that it is to be finished by tonight, and tomorrow morning on his way to school he'll take it. It's urgent..."

"Move, move, let me have a look," ordered the master.

Lal moved aside and waited like an owl in the dimly lit corner. His face was dry but he seemed to be torn between hope and despair. Old days of patting and derision possessed him.

"It's good. Happy that you're enriching your art day by day! Letters are awfully stylized, and people have to wear reading glasses to decipher your fingers. Of course you'll be praised! But leave it there, go to the far end, take that circular slab, and on it now ornately incise 'Madira Manzil'."

The master flung the burning butt of the cigarette into the busy road, took a napkin from his stainless cash box, and began to carefully clean two or three finished plates.

"But, babu, Headmaster will come with the sun rise. And he exhorts that he is a man of one word."

"Who is taller, headmaster or building contractor?"

"How can I tell? My eyes are failing."

"Think well. I mean, apply your common sense," cheerfully Madhu eyed Lal.

Lal pensively scratched head, blinked eyes, moved lips, and a while later said, "Contractor, babu."

"You're so cool, my old hand! Now you know why do I keep you even in difficult days?"

Lal beamed and went to the far end and took out a fine slab and began to polish it for etching the magic letters 'Madira Manzil'.

"Babu, how do I face the headmaster? He is a man of one word. Some troubles I sense at dawn, he'll peel off my skin out of my dying frame," Lal was visibly scared.

"Leave it on me, my old hand. Don't worry. I make him drink my water. What's wrong with a day delayed? It is not his daughter's marriage! He can easily wait a day. Hand me his nameplate meantime," annoyingly put Madhu.

Lal handed him the piece and argued no further with his master. He limped to the farthest corner and made busy himself with plate of the contractor.

"Lal, who is the man? A-b-u-l B-a-r-k-a-t! Is he a big politician or a great social reformer or a cricketer celebrity or a reality hero? This name sounds queer. Quite strange! In my whole life thousands of names crowd and vanish. But such an odd, smelly, bizarre name!" Madhu wore a sad face and threw a quizzical glance at Lal.

"Babu, what do we have with the man? Our task is to etch his name on the stone, and count coins. Is he dead or living? Is he a player or a torch bearer? Is he leader or a dealer? These and the likes are irrelevant to our sacred profession," flatly argued Lal.

"You claim that you are a primary drop-out, and you lecture like a pro-fe-ss-sor!" Madhu threw a fiery look. He felt uneasy with Lal's unsought exegesis.

"Sorry, babu," Lal cut his tongue, and next he paid double attention to his assigned work.

"Lal, let's come to the point. Let's debate logically. Headmaster and his stone can wait for another year. But how can we delay our boss's task. He is a big name in construction line. For ten long years he is building his palace with a swimming pool, a mini gym and an acre of sprawling flower garden. Crores he spends in this and that. Can he be waited? Have we the power to make him wait? We are too lucky, Lal. A client of his name and fame has graced our shack. Headmsater! Phoo! Many of his likes will come and go. Phoo! Can we delay boss's demand? No ways, Lal!"

"How can we?" Lal agreed with his master without taking his eyes off the egg-shaped slab.

Evening stealthily tiptoed, darkness thickened, and Lal under a tiny flickering bulb was fighting with his newly found friend. Tomorrow was the delivery date. And if he failed, his skin would be peeled off out of his body.

Next morning the headmaster, a clean shaven, glossy gentleman of fifty or so with a broad smile on his oval face stopped his alto just before the shed, and hurriedly asked for the nameplate. A room in his school was to be dedicated to the language martyr, Barkat, and a special lecture was to be delivered on his memory. He was in a hurry. Delegates would come from four corners of the state. A lot of arrangements had to be taken care of for the smooth passage of the hectic day.

"Where is my name-plate?" softly asked the headmaster looking around the stacked pillars of stones.

"Sir, it is almost finished. Please come tomorrow and take it easy," nonchalantly Lal said.

"Why?"

"Another urgent delivery, sir, from a big building contractor, who sleeps on sacks of raw notes. A crorepati! Fifty men he keeps for the upkeep of his house. Hundred engineers work under him! How can we delay his order? He is our patron, a friend in sun and shower, you know. "

The headmaster looked vacantly at the brilliant sky and looked for heavenly bodies for a minute.

"Where is your master?" calmly the headmaster asked.

"At home. May be sleeping still or taking rest. Yester night my master attended a big party. Tired, sir."

"Could you give his cell number?" the headmaster asked with a stifled tone.

"I have no mobile, sir," calmly clarified Lal.

"Would you take tea or coffee, sir?"

"No. Thanks."

Headmaster's face exuded a flush of anger, anxiety, remorse, and pity. He kept himself cool by forcibly repressing his strains of fear and inaction. He could not decide if he should wait or move snatching the unfinished piece of stone. In the end he lost his temper.

"How irresponsible you are! How do you run business with such an inert attitude? You have no sense, no ways to deal with clean people. It's terrible! It's horrific!" Headmaster burst in anger.

Nobody talked. Vehicles honked and speedily passed by the side of the shop.

"How much?" dryly asked the headmaster.

"Sir, it's unfinished. How can I deliver it?" indifferently Lal said.

"Stop. Not a word more. You are pollutants to people and places! Have you heard the name? Do you know the significance of the day? Okay, tell me today's date." Headmaster smashed.

"February 21."

"Good."

"Why do we celebrate it?"

"How can I tell? Me, a primary pass-out. Days come, days go. Orders we have, and signs we deliver. Beyond it I know nothing."

"Good! It's our fault, man. You have never heard the names of Salam, Barkat, Rafiq, Jabbar. Barkat was born at Babla village, Bharatpur, Murshidabad. And in his memory a room was donated by Sukhtara Bibi, an educationist, who is the chief guest of today's observance of International Mother Language Day at our school. Do you know history? No. Okay. On February 21, 1952, students of the University of Dhaka launched a nationwide protest against accepting Urdu as the nation's official language. In that peaceful protest Barkat and many other young boys were brutally killed. And in order to recognize and honour this heroic act, the United National Educational, Scientific and Cultural Organization (UNESCO) declared in 1999 February 21 as International Mother Language Day. It is a day of worldwide observance aimed at promoting multilingualism and awareness of both cultural and linguistic diversity." The Headmaster gasped, took the name-plate and with a light heart he departed.

Lal muttered for a while and sat sheepishly in that far end. How long? Who know?

❖❖❖

14

JABU'S RICKSHAW

At 10 in the morning the entry street to the Station B is packed with motley people and varied vehicles. It is the holy hour, the magic hour to the path of people's progress and prosperity. From early morning to late evening people from adjacent villages rush to the big City B to serve or to be served. And the cheap and best way to reach to town in time is by catching a train. A couple of up and down trains are fortunately scheduled to kiss the station at the gap of ten or twenty minutes at that happy hour. Sometime trains simultaneously come and depart both in platform no. 1 and 2. The station is then flooded with the waves of hurried people and the hubbub of the harrowing passengers fills the air.

The lane, however, lies empty at dawn. And at noon coolies idly sleep by its sides.

But at 10 the alley takes its magic and magnificient colour. Passengers – lively commuters, patients with children, the invalids and the aged, the job-seeking and ambitious young boys and girls, hawkers, masons, fruit-sellers, milk-sellers, lawyers, doctors, professors, buffaloes and cows and dogs – vie with vehicles – milk white scorpios or black boleros, pigmy altoes, bikes, scooters, cycles, vans, rickshaws. The lane is virtually choked for ten minutes. Anguished passengers abuse each other. Some sigh and rue and blame corporation officials for the encroachment of the lane by hawkers. Vehicles horn and honk without an end. People shout, jostle, elbow, shoulder, scuffle, and children, clutched to worried parents, cry in fear.

One day Jabu is caught in the mess. On his rusted rickshaw a tall, healthy young man cozily sits. He looks around and casually sees thousand angry faces barking, beating each other. And hequietly smokes. He is composed, cool, quiet, unpurturbed. His face is expressionless. It seems he is totally ignorant of his surroundings.

"Ei, rickshaw, pull, pull! You lazy rouge! Why don't you die, moron?" bursts a well-dressed, perfumed young man from his newly bought Enfield.

Jabu helplessly jerks and his rickshaw creaks and it moves just a step forward.

By Jabu's right hand a giant car, enshrined with flowery letter F, named after a five star city hotel, stands immobile. Nobody can see the driver or the passengers of the dark glassed vehicle. People look at the car in awe and mutter and gulp down their rage and fury in hush.

A lady from the opposite side of the lane shouts at Jabu, "Don't you have common sense? Why have you come here at this hour? People have no place to keep toes, and you, dull-headed, adds nuisance! Pull, pull! Why are you looking back? Brother, (she draws attention of a fellow passenger), am I wrong?"

The fellow, a muscular man with long curly hair, flung on his broad shoulder, agrees with her and they both charge Jabu for his crime. "Why don't you paddle on the main road? Don't you see it's a lane, narrow and congested? Who gives you permission to enter here?" the man asks and throws a repulsive glance at Jabu.

Jabu, aged over fifty, skeletal, sweaty in lungi and soiled shirt, feet naked, wears a quizzical look. It seems that he has lost words.

A battery-driven tuk tuk driver, is also stuck in the crowd, and tries hard to swim ashore. He is sweating profusely. Behind him a passenger anxiously sits in his car. He is to catch the train. Seconds pass, his face elongates more in tension. The driver suddenly jumps off his vehicle, fiercely catches the handle of Jabu's rickshaw, and somehow makes a space for the passage of his vehicle.

Jabu crouches in fear.

Meanwhile, a constable with a stick in his hand arrives on the spot. He surveys the chaotic scene, speaks nothing, charges his lathi randomly at the back of Jabu's rickshaw and berates him for his misdeed. Jabu is shaken and looks ashen. "What's my fault, sir?" he tearfully mutters.

The young man, calmly seated on the Jabu's rickshaw, lights another cigarette.

People, strangers and regulars, shopkeepers and garage-boys, praise the man in uniform for his timely service. The constable cracks a winning laughter and hastily moves towards the tea shop.

"Sir, you've acted on the occasion. These pullers are lice! They once sucked our blood. Now all they have vanished. A few oafs still skulk! Sir, why don't you drive them out of the city? They are eyesore to the beauty of our city," exhorts the shop keeper.

The constable agreeably grins.

The driver of the vehicle with letter F parks the car blocking the station gate. He bumps to the tea shop. The constable gaily shakes his hand, firmly takes him to his breast.

❖❖❖

15

KALI DASHI

A shining early morning.

A brood of birds quarrelled on the tin roof of Kali Dashi's hut. They vied to peck the scrubs of the stale bread Kali Dashi daily threw at dawn. For ten minutes they fought and caroused, and then disappeared one by one. The old Dashi then locked her hovel and began to trudge along the dusty village road for day's begging. Villagers called her Kali Dashi, as her skin looked like tar. Dashi lived in the remotest fringe of the village where shoe-makers, scavengers, sweepers, rag-pickers soothed day's wounds under the clusters of dazzling stars.

If one asked her age, she laughed like a child, and showed her blackish beautifully arrayed teeth. She had bushy grey hair, sharp nose, and small dark eyes. She was lean and of medium height. In her youth she was a village beauty. Now her skin slackened and shrank, and body wizened. Eyes lost luster, but her hair and teeth had still the remnants of her youthful exuberance.

Beside the jackfruit tree there were four rows of betel nuts, twirled with wild climbers, tossing heads in glee. The squirrels squeaked, birds sang, and monkeys chattered day long at her yard. And in spring cuckoos' carols made her tired. Mondays and Saturdays she didn't beg. She cooked whatever she had in store, and smoked biri and wasted time watching the swaying of the treetops. She heard the birds's song for hours and made war with the monkeys with her old oily crooked stick.

In summer days when the sun burnt everything to ashes Dashi lay under the shade of the jackfruit, and crooned. And when she sang, her dog Moti came from nowhere, and lay tucked to her caged ribs, and licked her cheeks wriggling its body and stirring tail. In winter she kept her shut for days. She didn't have regular bath or food. Only she smoked, and slept, and Moti howled now and then, and guarded the thatch. Her eyesight was poor, but ears were still sharp. She could sense a stranger even from a mile. Sometime she giggled, and next wept bitterly just like the alternate play of the sun and shower in a sparkling rainy day.

As a beggar she had a special status. She didn't beg with others, and never went to a door where once she was refused. And villagers if their hens or ducks or goats died, they waited for her turn. She tied and slung the dead ducks, hens or goats to one end of her walking stick, put it on her shoulder, and went home. And the children of the street followed her and taunted,

> *"O, Dashi, Khudar Khashi! Do you eat dead hens or rats? Give us the birds, we'll cook, and give you a cup of soup."*

And she hurled torrents of abuse, called their parents by obscene names. The children and the old alike relished the scene, and teased her more. She plodded, and children followed. She stopped, and children soon made them statues behind her back. They sometime threw dust and pelted her with fig fruits, tomatoes, and pebbles. And the dogs of our neighborhood barked and barked.

Maa loved Dashi much. On Sundays at our home Dashi along with a dozen of beggars were served with a pot of rice or coins. They were also offered old clothes, gunny sacks, plastic pots, vegetables, rice, eggs, milk, etc. From the early morning beggars made a beeline to our door. And we, the children of the house, quarrelled and skirmished to serve them first. Some wore lungis, and some dhotis. Women wore saris. Some were blind, some deaf and dumb, and came with their young hands. Some came limping. And the Muslims chanted 'la elaha illallah,' and the Hindus 'hare krishna, hare ram,' by playing flutes or beating drums. They queued, had alms and, blessed us for Allah's and Bhagawan's bounty and bliss.

There was a yearly ritual at our home. In every year a Friday was fixed for the feast of the beggars. On that holy day they came well dressed. We hardly recognized them. They gossiped, dined, and belched, took shelter at an attached shed. They then sang some of their own, some form other noted pirs and bauls, and recited special verses from the holy books, and asked gods for our good health and wealth. They blew on our heads, lovingly tapped cheeks, and prayed. The elders all circled them, and we became dumb with awe and wonder. Maa wiped her eyes, and father and uncles looked grave and solemn.

On that day Dashi used to come in her best white sari. She didn't dine with other guests. She sat on our verandah and smoked biri. Maa called her then, and she followed to the kitchen. She was offered a sack to sit cross legged, a palm leaf to fan, and served food on a banana leaf. She didn't speak. When we went close to her, she looked at us with the eyes of a timid rabbit. After eating she went to the side of the well. She sat under our guava tree, smoked, and dozed for a while. And when the sun mellowed, she took whatever maa gave her as gift, and slogged homeward.

Sometime in some hot summer days she sat under a kadam tree after the day's round. The tree was in full bloom, and its scent wafted the village. Birds were flinging from twigs to twigs, and their callings made peasants fatigued. They clamped hands in exasperation, but the birds took no flight. They kept mum for a while, and sang again. Dashi used to haunch at a farthest corner, and smoked languidly. Meanwhile the urchins got the news of Dashi's arrival, and they soon rounded and humiliated her with filthy words and lewd gestures. An elderly man or woman, however, drove the children away, and rescued her for the day.

And the day when nobody came, exasperated by the children she cried, and thumped her head against the kadam tree. And if her anger was not assuaged, she threw her sari away and made her stark naked. Children fled, men took their eyes off, and then from somewhere an aunt came running, and tried to wrap her around. She shrieked and fought her, and shook her aged body vehemently. She then looked wild. She laughed terribly. She whirled and whirled until she fell flat on the ground. She squeezed, and threw her limbs at every side. She pulled her hair, and groaned like a wounded animal. She became smeared with dust, and a strain of thick saliva oozed out of her wasted lips.

Nobody knew her story. But the elderly said she was once married to a famous Kaloo dacoit. He abused her for days, and tied her often to a post. He didn't give her food either. People feared Kaloo and shunned him. They lamented for Dashi but couldn't do anything. And at one dead of night when the moon was bathing the village and the paddy fields looked silvery, she somehow untied herself. Her husband was in deep sleep. She took a knife, and sliced him into pieces. That night her neighbours couldn't sleep. Dogs whined, foxes squeaked, and children cried spasmodically throughout the night. And in the morning when the dogs and foxes clashed for the flesh, villagers crowded, and culled the pieces into a sack and burnt it in a nearby crematory.

Years later one day, Dashi, hair gray, limbs twisted, body bent, appeared at the village with some dead hens. She cleared the abandoned hut, built a mud oven, and cooked, and a foul smoke engulfed the village. Villagers were vexed, and cursed her, and impatiently counting days for her death. But death eluded her, and she lived for another decade.

Then the year of the deluge came. The river swelled and swallowed the village. Huts and cattle were washed away. Many died. A few took shelter to some upper lands. We made rafters of banana, and swam across the village at day. And at night we took shelter in a big two storied house of a rich man. People forgot to eat, and they all cursed Dashi for their bad luck. Some had lost cattle, some children, some huts and dogs. Water was everywhere. There was no place for burial or burning the dead. Corpses of cats, dogs, birds, children, elderly, and cattle were floating on the flooded river day and night.

We couldn't burn Dashi. We placed the corpse onto a rafter, and wrapped her with leaves of banana, and tied it with ropes, and let it go with the surge of the slimy whirling eddies.

❖❖❖

16

MAA

"How are you, my friend?" I merrily asked while basking in the morning sun.

Amzad dryly laughed, "Going on somehow." His words were stale, dry, and lifeless. I was hurt and gaped, "What a change!" My cheerfulness got a severe jolt.

Amzad was my classmate at Patikabari High School. We spent days together playing football and kabadi, flying kites in afternoons, sharing tiffin at tiffin breaks, visiting each other's home at festivals. Later I moved to Kolkata and he graduated from our local Amtala College. He had an elder brother, a school headmaster, who shifted with his family to Berhampore, our district town. Meantime Amzad's father died of heart arrest and his mother out of shock lost her mind. Dr Hassan, a famous psychiatrist of our town expressed his helplessness about her recovery.

With insane mother at home and no suitable job in hand Amzad has set up his own shoe store at Patikabari market. He follows a strict schedule – with *fajr* azan(early morning prayer) he leaves bed, tidies rooms, makes breakfast, cooks dishes, changes his mother, combs her hair, feeds her, makes her cozily sit at her chair, washes dishes and clothes, locks her up and runs towards his store. At noon he closes his shop, runs to his home and spends afternoons with her. In the evening he opens his store for two hours or so. Nights often keep him stand at her bedside. Buyers were unhappy. Many regulars stopped visiting his store. His business was badly hit for irregularity of service.

"He can keep an aaya, is it a big issue?" You're fair. But it is a village. Hired aayas or nurses or maids are not available. And neighbourhood women are nowhere. They all have gone to Delhi, Mumbai and other big cities to make their fortune.

So he decided not to marry and pass his days serving his mad maa.

"How is your maa?" casually he asked me while taking out a box from one of the upper racks.

Amzad in our school days often visited our home and maa liked him as her son. We dined together, played together. Sometime he passed night at our home.

"Well," I said, "going somehow. There is no chronic ailment, no specific disease, only old age infirmity and weakness of bones."

"Who takes care of your maa?"

I was not happy with his query, but I didn't lose my way. He could ask me about my children, their upbringing and passions. He could ask me about my salary as the old faces and friends of my village usually did whenever I visited my ancestral home. But about maa...

"Why! My brothers! We are five. They are quite well off. Moreover, they live at village. They have free time. What the villagers do? Eat and sleep! So to my brothers my maa is not a burden, and she is also happy with familiar faces and known surroundings."

"You take no care of your mother? Okay, I understand. Have you taken her to your Berhampore home?" teasingly Amzad put. I was upset with his sudden jibe.

"No. I send monthly money for her. Why will I keep her caged in my six hundred square feet box? I don't want to uproot an old tree. She will, I fear, lose her liveliness at my place. Her roots will dry and branches will be leafless, I think. We live at fifth floor. There are four neighbours – a deeply engaged aged couple who routinely visit hospitals; an aged widower, egoistic-babbler and a howler; a Marwari who counts coins seven days a week and a loveless widow who has lost her mind. Doors are opened, doors closed, sounds are hollow, empty, too tiresome! It's so calculative, mechanical, and artificial life! So boring! We have jobs and we live in hurry. Rat race you know. We have no time to read the lines of old faces. My maa is firmly rooted in dust and soil. How could she live on clean, glossy stones with no work in hand? T.V. she hates. People she seeks for her pastime. Where can I find men or women who will talk of milking cows, parrots and sparrows, wheat fields, acacia trees, swirling Jalangi, fishing boats, calm sunset or brilliant sunrise?"

Amzad looked confused and fitfully scratched his head for a while. He put on a queer face. His face did betray neither joy nor pain.

I read a line from a poem to assuage my pain. It was like this – *ami thaki choto ghore boro mon loye, nijer dukkher anno khai sukhi hoye* (I live at a hut with an oceanic mind, happily I eat food of my sorrow). I bend the line to suit it to my tenor – *ami thaki boro ghore choto mon loye, nijer sukher anno khai dukhi hoye* (I live in a palace with a mean mind, sadly I eat the food of my joy."

Amzad was not a poet. He was a shoe-seller. It dawned in me a little later, and I swallowed bitter pills of my misdeed. This was not the first time. I did it often. I could not check the temptation of reading out a poem. That time I forgot about the audience. I had read poetry before lawyers, doctors, engineers, tax officers, educationists, deans, doyens, principals, peons, school masters and text book writers, academicians, social reformers and I had now mastered the art of silence. But old habits hardly died. So today again I was punished with my own morbid voice.

"Good! My learned friend! You haven't mortgaged your maa at old home. I am so happy for you. I know your pain. You are a city-dweller now. You have to maintain standards of city-life. Your wife, you, your children – all are busy, rushing and rushing round the clock. Where is the time for an old, useless scrap at your furnished 2 BHK?"

"Water."

Amzad offered a bottle from a dark corner. I drank and wiped forehead with my arms.

"How much?" hurriedly I asked taking the box of slippers from his colourless hand.

"Two hundred fifty," he claimed.

"Come in one afternoon. Take a look at my mother. She will not figure out your face. But she needs your prayer. Come and take tea with us. Maa will be happy to see you," earnestly Amzad asked.

"Of course I'll come. After all your maa is my maa too. Bye, friend. See you in the afternoon."

I could not keep my promise. A year passed. One evening Daku, another friend from my village, called me and informed me of Amzad's orphanage.

I sent my deep condolence from the over-crowded waiting chamber of a pediatrician.

❖❖❖

17

ORPHANED ONCE AGAIN

"Who is there?" asked a stranger in a nasal voice from a thicket at the outskirts of the forest.He was gasping for breath.

"It's me, the watchman of the cemetery. But who are you? Who is the devil at this evil hour?" shrilly riposted the old watchman. "Uh…the winds rage and the clouds burst. The lightning blinds eyes. Boughs bend to the hedges, and the devil is after me, uh…."

An aged, rickety, bearded man, shabbily clothed, scurried through the nettles and pleaded with folded hands, "Pardon me, sir! O, the howling winds, raving clouds! Have pity on the orphan, sir! I've lost my way in the wilderness."

"Eh! Who are you?" agitatedly asked the watchman while twitching his slackened cheeks.

"An orphan who has lost his way in the storm," repeated the stranger in the same nasal voice. He looked harrowed.

"No orphanage here, man!" gibed the old caretaker and next he indulgently assured, "but don't worry, friend. You are at home! Feel cool at my cozy corner. Moreover, I'm a keeper of a friendlier home, an acre of burial ground. Cheer up, friend! Welcome to an untrammelled patch of long grass and scented weeds."

The watchman took the stranger to his crooked hut. The stranger bent and entered the shack and stealthily scanned the gloomy corners. The hovel was empty. A hurricane was furtively flickering at a corner. There was no furniture, no utensils. No traces of living at all! Strange! The stranger looked upset.

Both sat on a sack on the mud floor and smoked biri. Rains pitter-pattered on the tin roof. Outside it was hoary and dark. The winds groaned and moaned. The forest from time to time flashed with the lightning.

"So, friend, how do you lose your parents?" soberly asked the watchman while placing a pinch of snuff into his nostrils.

The stranger coughed, waved hands before his face and grudged, "Who says I have lost parents. O, heavens! They are hale and hearty! They run a chicken farm with the aid of a local boy and make quick bucks in seasons. O foul-mouthed, evil-eyed old haggard! God saves your nasty soul!"

"But you say you are an orphan," feebly protested the watchman with a baffled look.

"So I am!" claimed the stranger with animation. His face flushed and eyes gleamed.

"How?" the watchman plainly asked and argued, "An orphan is a child whose parents are dead. Am I wrong?"

"Am I a child?" the stranger quizzically asked and thoughtfully stroked his grey, short beard.

"No, you are almost close to grave!" solemnly said the watchman.

"My words you borrow," plainly put the stranger and demanded, "touch me and say a truth. Perhaps you are afraid of pure truths which God prescribes. Why do you waste your life juggling with man-made words? Pooh!" He looked irritated and casually asked for another smoke.

"Stop babbling at my sacred yard," blared the watchman. "Do you think I am a fool? Once I was a gentleman, polished and perfumed, serving men of power and pomp in big houses. But by the fun of fate I am destined to watch a graveyard now." His voice was choked and eyes teary.

"I don't differ," nodded the stranger and poorly protested, "I only claim that orphans need not be only fatherless or motherless. At my age a widower is an orphan! My parents are fine with their farm. But my heart, my love, my life reached heaven yesteryear." He looked ashen and extremely weak. His eyes were teary. He hopelessly flung the dead butt of the biri to a corner and asked again for a smoke.

"Get out of my hut," the watchman yelled in fury, "who is an orphan, you or me? Eh... if you are an orphan, triply I'm so! My parents were dead, wife was dead, and my children drove me out of my own house. The village headman showed mercy and kept me to guard this damned yard. And here in this cheerless maze a lone sulking soul is stinking! How many years? Have you any idea?" boomed the watchman contemptuously and he looked fiery.

A silence followed.

The winds meantime ceased. The rains also slowed a bit. The sky was still overcast. Frogs croaked around, fireflies danced over the shrubbery and yonder beetles shrilly sang without an end. A skulk of foxes squeaked somewhere in the forest.

"But, brother, don't mourn for your loss. It's normal," the watchman broke his silence and sought to palliate the stranger's pain, "or in other way, there is nothing to grieve. And in God's world nobody is orphan. At our age we can't marry again! So keep quiet and coolly pass the residual days. Moreover, here waits our welcoming home. It's luxurious, fenced with long grass and fragrant flowers. There is also the shade of overhanging yew trees."

"Are you a priest or a watchman?" huskily asked the stranger and darted the dead butt and inspected the dim hut again. "Not even a bronze glass or a plate or a stack of logs!" he muttered and moaned.

"Are you parched?" the watchman affectionately asked.

"No," the stranger curtly said.

For a minute nobody spoke further.

The rains again began to patter on the tin. Suddenly a torch flashed nearby and a man whistled. The stranger sprang to his feet and hastily ran towards the forest.

"Hey, where are you parting at this ruffled hour? Hey! Ahoy! Don't move." The watchman gawkily followed the stranger skirting the soggy weeds with his stick. His legs were unsteady.

"Ruffled night is our friend, man. Keep watching your home. Again we meet if God wishes!" the stranger shouted from a safe distance and speedily receded into the forest.

The watchman panted and fumbled for his way. The wick of his sooty lantern abruptly died. He smelt evil in the dark.

He lay sleepless whole night. Thousand vicious thoughts crowded his restless soul. When cocks crowed in the village, he hobbled to the yard. And one by one he checked the graves.

Yes, his fear came true! The nubile girl who hanged herself a week ago was dug out of her grave.

In the afternoon the headman called an urgent meeting with the villagers. A decision was unanimously taken. The poor watchman was readily dismissed for the neglect of his assigned duty.

The poor old watchman became orphaned once again.

❖❖❖

18

OUR CARETAKER

Nagen Das is our caretaker. We have replaced 'Das' with 'Da' and lovingly call him Nagen Da. Elderly members of our society, however, call him by his name. Aged around sixty, tall, slim, fair, duty-bound, Nagen Da is a man of many parts. He is a mechanic and can repair fan, motor, fridge. At times he takes one day leave. That day he gives a stall in a village fair. He sells parched nuts, makes money, and buys dolls and sweet for tiny members of his home. Next day again he joins us.

Before Nagen Da's recruitment we have a harrowing time. People, young, middle aged, elderly were regularly recruited. But a week or two they served, and then disappeared. And they could not take care of themselves. How could they take care of fifty people? One day we saw a young boy who at 10 a. m. was peacefully snoring reclining on his chair at the gate of our block. The record book lay idle in the table. Another day we saw an aged man smoking biri and checking bags of owners and strangers alike. People complained. We called our agency and next day he was relieved. Then again a middle aged widower took care of us. He talked and talked, and had a keen interest in our personal lives. So he was freed. This way in five year a hundred men we have hired and fired.

Then one day rains go away, the sky becomes clear and the sun shines. Nagen Da arrives, and within a month we begin to depend on him. Working parents are not at home. Nagen Da takes the boy or girl to home. A flat owner has gone to visit a temple, and the milkman has come. He rings and manages the milk. Letters, papers, magazines, and bills he carefully keeps in his custody. And soon he see us, he hands them over. If a room is locked and a teacher has come, he does his best. A cook has come, and nobody is at home, he coughs and clears the air.He helps the delivery boys light their load.

In early morning his routine is to switch the pump on, to switch the lights off, and to unlock the front gate and the gate of the roof, to welcome a dozen delivery boys, bearers, sweepers, cooks, maids, and drivers. Every morning he cleans cycles and bikes, and earns some paise extra. He greets us with 'good morning' and 'good night' and we also return the same with broad smile on our face.

One evening I saw Nagen Da spreading some crumpled newspapers in a corner of our garage. The basement was empty. I, two LED bulbs, two lizards on the ceiling aiming at worms, one frog under a car, a dozen cockroaches, and a swarm of mosquitoes were the audience, and Nagen Da was the lone actor.

"Nagen Da, what's the matter? Why are you covering the dust with papers while the chairs are empty?" I asked in a bewildered voice.

Nagen Da bashfully smiled while warily caressing the creased papers in an obvious attempt to straighten them.

"It's pleasant time. Surroundings are quiet. I only want to make it more pleasant," Nagen Da laughed like a child.

I was confused. Mosquitoes were hovering over heads. They were biting hard. So I randomly moved my limbs, scratched the wounds and walked round the shady garage.

Minutes later he turned up with a set of tabla kept well in two worn out bags coated with a thick layer of dust.

"Is it a gift?" I asked with a smile.

Nagen Da looked at me with an expression which did not openly confirmed 'yes' or 'no'. He took a piece of cloth and began to clean the bags sitting cross-legged on the paper.

The frog at regular interval came out of the shadow of the car, caught a worm and playfully returned back to the shadow again.

"Nagen da, where is the mosquito coil?" I thumped my legs and asked.

"Finished," he dully said.

"How? Yesterday I bought it, and you have burnt them all! Not a broken one you save? No, it's bad," I vexed.

"Dada, do you know Voju?" indifferently he asked.

"Who is Voju?" I riposted.

"Why? The black man with yellowish tiger-teeth whom you one day gave a smoke. Remember that angular face, that lanky man who comes here every other evening and talks of fishing and fields. That fellow is my childhood friend, Voju."

"So!"

"Dada, he is a caretaker of Shanti Niwas. He asks for a coil and steals the whole packet. Stealing is in his blood. In childhood he made a name in our neighbourhood Kurmatuli by stealing. He stole eggs of birds and chickens, marbles, fish, bananas, guavas, mangoes, wood apples and so. In one full moon winter night he led us to the river bank. He climbed the date trees one by one like a monkey, and took off the rasa-filled pitchers. We merrily drank and danced together that night." He took the tiny hammer and began to beat the side strings of the tablas.

I felt elated but feigned that I was not happy with the loss of the coils.

"Dada, it's not a gift," Nagen Da clarified, "I have bought them at Rs. 500. I think I make a bargain," he beamed.

For a fortnight or so Nagen Da lost his cheerfulness. He looked pale and wan. He was no longer a talker. Day and night he sat in his chair, moved lips, looked at the ceiling, and watched the lizzards catching worms. The known faces smelt odd at his changed ways. Perhaps a loss in the family! Perhaps a quarrell with family members or friends or neighbours! Perhaps a thought of dowry for daughter's marriage!

Then one evening I saw him again sitting on the papers with his tablas. They looked new, and the bol was too good.

"Nagen Da, you have really made a bargain at Rs.500!" I merrily added.

He threw a resigned look and tiredly said, "Playing tabla is my passion from childhood. It's a disease within. What can be done? I spend on it Rs. 3000 more. For a poor caretaker like me it is a luxury! Family members, friends, relatives are angry and they've stopped speaking to me."

"They are not fools, I think," opined I.

Nagen Da slowly measured me from head to toe. His eyes were keen, and apparently there was hatred and derision in his look.

"I've always taken you as an exception. A genial man! But I am mistaken. You too wear the furs of the fretful earthlings! You have no wings to soar. And happy with your home and hearth!" he rued and spat. He looked terribly sad.

A car entered. Nagen Da sprang up, made passage for it by crumbling the corners of his papers, saluted Dr. Dutta, and when the doctor made his way to the lift, he again spread the papers and sat and began to beat.

I took a chair and watched him playing. He felt uneasy.

"Leave me alone. Go home and watch a reality show with boudi. Or visit a lottery shop and catch the moon. Why do you waste your valuable time here? It's a useless art and only fit for a useless few!" he lashed.

"I need to go to shop a packet of salt," I defended.

"Then go. If you are late you'll lose salt, and have to go empty at night," he threw a loathing glance at me.

Nagen Da looked serious. He briskly hammered the tablas while muttering himself, fiercely killed a mosquito, fixed his gaze at the peeping frog for a while, and then began to play again.

❖❖❖

19

RENDEZVOUS WITH A LEADER

"Hey! Rise, rise! Don't snore. Rush to the river. Meantime, I add fire to the oven," said Zarina shaking and lovingly thumping his man who lay half-naked on the mud floor. The day was extremely hot, and the night merciless. People perspired in profusion day and night. Frequent baths gave them only a fleeting relief.

Jabbar yawned and wallowed. He then stood up with a jerk, and his eyes fell straight on the stunning portrait of the ever smiling leader. It was aptly hung in the middle of the wall. The neta was tall, bald, nose sharp, cheeks glossy, and eyes brilliantly shinning. Suddenly he flung the napkin on the floor, rushed to the portrait, kissed it again and again and muttered, "O! My leader! O! Our leader! Years we cherish to touch your feet, and today our dream turns into a reality!"

And like the days of the festival villagers from early morning swam in the river, dressed their best, and queued before the bus. For window-seats they cried and clashed. The scene was extraordinary. It happened once in a blue moon. The bus would leave at 9 a.m. from A M High School ground.

It was mid-May. Today the leader of national repute would address a gathering in the district town. The roads leading to the Kranti Maidan were polished, and the trees and poles of both sides of the roads were wrapped with the party flags, festoons, cut outs and hoardings. The flags were fluttering at the whisk of wayward wind. Passers-by all wore a cheerful look. The offices and the shops were almost deserted. Villagers crowded each street, and they were shouting slogans and milling mirthfully toward the Maidan.

"Where's my son?" coughed and asked an elderly party worker, a farmer, a tall, lean man, a widower of the village.

"Oh! Father, take the stool, he's coming. Take a cup of tea, meantime," insisted Zarina pulling veil over her face, and the oven was belching smoke, thick blackish, grey.

"No urgent need maa. Another day I'll come. Just tell my boy to take the festoon to be pasted on the front of the bus. Ah! Forty rainless days, and this blistering heat!" the old peasant got up and trudged toward his fence, wiping beads of sweat from his forehead with a napkin lousily poorly hanging from his scraggy neck.

The bus was packed like a tin of sardines. The workers yelled for half an hour. And when the tide of initial excitement ebbed away, they searched for the driver. They were vexed. And they abused parents of the driver by swearing his hundred evil names. Then a gaunt man, with blunt nose, reddish hair, over-drunk, came tumbling and began to honk as loudly as he could. The conductor hallooed, boomed the bus thrice and it began to roll with a heavy jerk. Passengers fell on each other. And they began to abuse the man in charge. A thick smoke and dust free flowed around.

"Uncle, it's a lifetime chance!" beamed Jabbar. His eyes were tinkling, and ears red.

"Yes, Jabu," nodded the aged man solemnly while pressing tobacco on his scabbard palm. He thumped the tobacco dust thrice and offered a pinch to Jabu, and looked at outside scenes.

The houses and trees were gleefully running behind. And through the open window dusty air covered the old man, and he soon felt drowsy.

"Uncle, it's only morning, and you're sleeping!" cried Jabu impatiently and blabbered, "look at the ponds, fields, houses, shops, children! It's beautiful, full of life! Nobody hangs blinders before our eyes. It's freedom! Ah! Allah is gracious!"

"You're not a palaver! I suppose. You are a farmer. You have deep roots!" the man uttered with lips tight, and again he fell asleep. And a minute later he straightened himself to the seat and blared, "Jabu, is it the first time you see fields, ponds, cattle, kilns, children, beggars? Huh! And for freedom who is in chains? *Goras* (British) left decades ago. Why does the question of freedom arise? Our land is free! We are free! You can go wherever you like, and do what you like! Close eyes. The day isn't for chattering! Don't distrb. Let's me sleep for a while."

The bus lumbered past the festooned road. Newly fastened flags were fluttering, and the life size cut outs of the leader were seen everywhere and he seemed to be blessing people with holy hands. Party activists from the hood of the bus shouted slogans, battered drums, clapped hands and sang in unison, and waved hands to the passers-by and occasionally made lewd gestures to a passing rustic girl or a fat housewife.

Finally the bus stopped with a jerk at a corner of the Kranti Maidan. The sun was overhead. The field was flooded with all sorts of vehicles, and the people were excited like the fanatics of our land. A group was moving this side another that side, women screaming, children crying, hawkers hawking *chanas* and plastic toys, balloons. Villagers urinated under the bush, and on the sands. Their motley attires gave the city a sudden raffish look. City men looked at the poor folks as if they were men of circus, and just freed from its tent!

"Uncle, uncle, we're at Kranti Maidan. Let's brush quickly," Jabu said with anxiously and briskly fumbled for his pocket mirror. He combed, dusted from head to toe, and made him ready for the long cherished rendezvous.

"Oh! The bus is empty as a broken haat! Where have they all gone leaving us in the lurch, Jabu?" rued the old man.

"Why? They all blare and you snore like a fat drunkard! You are a nonchalant old haggard, and you claim yourself a party worker! Tell me why have you come in the town? What's night for? Phoo!" indignantly Jabu queried, and spat through the window.

"Calm my boy, calm! Give ears to the speakers. Why shall we hurry?" coldly argued the old man, and put a betel leaf into his mouth and rolled it quietly with his tongue.

"Ok! Sleep at the bus then! I'm going..." Jabu angrily said and hurriedly came out of the bus. He set his feet on the dust, and his eyes glistened. A sea of people was waving through the sprawling sands. The ground was abuzz with the varied shouting, chanting, and slogans. Mikes blared, vehicles horned. And the leader was yet to arrive. The dais was wrapped with festoons and flags and flowers. A bevy of beauties were waiting to touch the feet of the leader, and be blessed for life!

"Hey! Stop. Don't' move a pace further, raise hands skyward," grinned a tall, well-built three starred uniformed man, and immediately a swarm of young constables with bamboo poles in hands rushed to Jabu, and carried him to the police corner.

"Who're you?" mockingly asked a young constable.

"Ja...Jabbar...Sir."

"Oh! A Bangladeshi, I see!"

"No, Sir, me from Sonamukhi village. Truth I tell. Not a word I lie. Believe me," pleaded Jabbar with folded hands.

"Show aadhar card then," casually the constable asked.

"I forget it, sir."

"It's okay. Voter card please."

"I don't have the original. But a photocopy..." Jabbar fumbled one of his hind pockets, and took out a crumpled paper.

"Take it sir."

"What's it?"

"Voter card."

"No photocopy. Show the original," coldly said the constable while sipping juice in a cane.

Both were silent for a while.

"Okay, what you do, Babar?" enquired the constable again.

"Me not Babar, sir. I'm Jabbar."

"Oh! Sorry! What you do Jabar?"

"A farmer sir," benignly he said.

"How much land do you have?" mechanically asked the constable.

"Not a decimal sir. I am a landless farmer. The landed peasants hire me in season, and in off season I work as a mason's hand in Gujrat, Bengaluru, Kerala."

"Why have you come here then?" the constable calmly asked.

"I am part-time party worker sir, and I love our leader. It's my dream to meet him. And Allah opens eyes, and the chance comes today. I'll go and handshake with my leader. From the day his arrival is announced, sleep eludes me. Please let me go sir. In a minute our leader will come. Please sir, please," Jabbar said at a sweep, and knelt before the constable. Under the sweltering heat his voice turns dry, hoarse, and weak.

"Hey! Chatka, come quick, take him to the corner and tie him to a pole," ordered the constable, and the water- man dragged him to the corner.

Meanwhile the leader arrived escorted by thousands of police officers garnished with state of the art guns and he delivered his golden speech. People were enthralled, and they made wounds on their palms by continuous clapping. For half-an hour the city looked a cemetery. The shops were shuttered, and in offices some old clerks were dozing under the whirring fans. Even the street dogs were not found; a week long special drive was jointly carried out by the municipality and local police station to make the city dogs-free. Birds left days before. Only some jackdaws were still clambering in a nearby heap of leftover where flies incessantly buzzing and feasting.

"Please sir, please, let me go…time is running out…," bid Jabbar with tears in his eyes.

"Don't cry. It's forbidden. People come here to cheer!" warned the water-man.

"Let me go sir. If not on the dais I can touch his feet, please let me have a full look at our leader. And I'll slave you for life," cajoled Jabbar.

"What?"

"Slave sir. I mean servant sir."

"Who needs a servant at home? I am a servant," the water-man looked confused.

"Okay, let that go. Please give your hand, sir."

"Why? Are you a palmist?"

"Yes sir, a bit..."

"Fine, tell then what waits ahead...?"

"Yes, uh...have a beautiful wife, and she cooked well, father mother dead, sister widowed, a neighbouring boy tries to make inroad into her life in your absence...big danger, fire lies here...." murmured Jabbar cautiously studying the lines of the water-man's palms.

"Danger! What danger?" the water-man sprang to his feet, as if a tongue of fire caught him.

"No need to worry sir. A way I find..." Jabbar laughed a harmless laugh.

"Sir, you go home at nine and come at early morning. Right?"

"Right. Doing it for last ten years. It's usual," claimed the water-man.

"Usual it was then, when your parents acted as guards, and your widowed sister had not fled with the butcher from your home. It's unusual now," Jabbar thumped him forcibly. "Okay, give me a smoke, I'm dying for it."

"It's forbidden here," claimed the water-man.

"Ah! Crying is forbidden here, smoking forbidden here! How do you live here, man, no, sir?" languishingly he anguished.

"Try not to play clever. What's the way out?"

"Oh! I forget it," Jabbar scratched head, and his eyes fixed on the ground. He kept silent for five minutes, and claimed, "Difficult sir, arduous task. Let's see."

"Okay, do you love your wife?"

"Each night we made love like hens."

"Night…?" fiercely Jabbar asked, and shook the water-man in sheer rage. Then next he became a child again and urged, "Hear me first, then reply. You're a nice young man and have a beautiful wife at home, you agreed earlier. Am I wrong?"

"No."

"Okay, keep eyes on my eyes, and confide, "Does your wife love you alike?"

"Yes."

"How do you know?"

"Why? Her belly day by day is ballooning."

"That's bliss. Please visit home at some awkward noon, and make love. You know days compliment nights. And if you are burnt then, pine not. That's the ways of life, sir!"

"What do you mean, man?" flabbergasted he was.

"I mean what I mean. Fencing around a beautiful garden is good! But watering and weeding out the weeds are welcome moves! Oh! You're sweating profusely. Be aired and cool, sir."

The water-man hurriedly untied and knelt before Jabbar.

Jabbar dusted himself, and rushed to the milling crowd.

When he swam ashore, leader left the dais, and he was being escorted by hundreds of sleek, milky white dark-glassed cars. And the crowd was waving and waving behind. Some eyes shone brilliant, and some were shaded with shards of tears.

Jabbar retreated to an empty corner, littered with used bottles, crumpled papers, discarded plastic cups. The sands whirled at the thrash of million feet, and the Maidan was hazy, smoky, dark, and lurid. He saw the waves of the people, and he suddenly felt as light as a feather.

The darkness soon wrapped the field, and the sands were cold. The bus no 2139 was ready to roll. But Jabbar didn't come. The old man guarded the seat for his nephew. Good and evil thoughts were alternately playing on his mind. Standing party workers were intoxicated, jubilant, and garrulous. They kept eyes on the Jabbar's empty seat with a vulture's eyes.

Then the old man shrieked, and the workers were shaken to the marrow. He shoved away the passengers and warned the driver not to inch a stride.

He rummaged the field alone, and found him lying swooned, and his body was smeared with dust and sweat. He cried, a most horrible cry, and the co-passengers rushed toward the corner. He sprinkled waters on his face, and patted him. Some messaged limbs and others stomach. Then slowly Jabbar came to life.

Next morning he slept till noon. Zarina rose early when the cocks crowed. She bathed, cooked, swept the yard. She tossed his man and pleaded, "O, my man! Why do you hide from the sun? It's blazing outside, and the river rippling. Rise and swim, and tell your story. Have he hugged you? Have you touched his feet, and been blessed?"

Jabbar tightly pulled his legs and head close to his breast, and muttered for a while, and lay like a twisted log. For how long did he dream or sleep ? Only Zarina can tell.

❖❖❖

20

SHERMAN'S HOUSE

Dr. Misra confirmed that the patient would die within ten days. The news spread across the village like a wild fire. People from far and near made a beeline to Sherman's house from early hour of the day. They queued before Sherman's gate to have a last look at the dying man. The house was abuzz with the noise of people's constant coming and going. A shade of tarpaulin was readily made for the shelter of the well-wishers. It was at the backwoods of the big white house. A mango grove and a big pond kept the makeshift shade cool and cozy.

Sherman was a respectable man. He had thirty acres of fertile land. He married twice. When the first wife Sakina failed to give him a boy, people pleaded him to marry again. And thus he married Jarina who is not as beautiful as Sakina. She was black, tall and healthy, and much younger and, gave Sherman five sons. His sons were all established. They lived in different Indian cities. They came home to see the face of their father for the last time. Big cars lined before the gate, and children in expensive clothes continuously ran in and out of Sherman's house like colourful butterflies. The neighbours were all rugged folks, the peasants and the poor. And to them Sherman's house turned into a joyous place of rest and comfort.

Villagers ceased working at fields for days. They passed time at Sherman's instead. Some brought fresh ripe fruits; some brought fresh vegetables, some milk, fish and meat. They did it willingly. Such respect and love Sherman had in the village Mehedipur.

Peasants were in general barred from entering into the interior of the Sherman's house. If a visitor wanted to meet Sherman, he would have to wait at his designated chamber. Only the respectable and the wealthy people had an occasional entry. But now the door was open to all. Known, unknown faces swarmed and circled the dying bed. In the early hours people were thin. But as the sun shone bright, the crowd thickened. The four sides of the bed were fixed for four kinds of people. At the head side sat Sakina and Jarina, both weeping and reciting the verses from the Quran. The leg side was reserved for the sons and their wives. And two other sides, the left reserved for the village women and the right for the village men. Incense sticks were repeatedly burning and dying in a distant corner, and the ashes smeared the floor round the incense vase.

"Sherman once was a *sher* (tiger). He killed bisons, rhinos, elephants in the Kahardinga forest at dead of night. He never shot birds, deer and other lowly animals, and he hated company. Alone he roamed and killed wild beasts. He killed not for money but to challenge the animals to cower him. Such charismatic figure he was. Tall and black with chiseled body and sharp black eyes, hair hung to his broad shoulders, a cut mark on the left cheek he was a man to be feared. People usually shunned him. He was a great wrestler and a great swimmer too. And in matters of feuds what he said was right. Nobody dared to disagree," narrated an old peasant who smoked and coughed and spat, sitting on haunches at the side of Sherman's pond. His face was shrunk, and body wizened. The day was hot, and air stopped blowing. The old man with the end of his napkin wiped the beads of sweat from his face. And he now began to whir it around his bald head.

So the people like ants made a beeline, and were coming in and going out of the white house day and night. Peasants stopped harvesting, and their women stopped cooking, and the children were running merrily in and around Sherman's house. Sherman's health, meantime, deteriorated day by day. His sons lost hope. Famous city doctors failed. People told them to call fakirs, yogis, and so they were called. They came and nursed Sherman with their water, oil, and other liquids for three days. They messaged the patient, murmured mantras for hours, and gave special neem-bath. The patient felt good in the morning. He could talk, drank a cup of juice, and slept for an hour in the afternoon. But as the sun reclines in the west, the pain gripped him again. And so one day the fakirs and yogis also lost hope. They took rewards and left. And people taunted them as fake fakirs and yogis.

Sherman had no fever, no breathing problem. His heart beat was normal. But he could neither sit nor lie for five minutes at a stretch. His sons always sat beside him, and made him sit and lie at fixed intervals. When he sat, he groaned in pain, and his elder son made him lie. And when he lay he moaned again, and his youngest son made him sit. For ten days thus Sherman suffered. And at dead of night when people thinned, and his tired sons and exhausted wives took a nap, Sherman himself did this rhythmic gymnastics of sitting and lying with the help of two iron chains hung from the ceiling. The killer pain made Sherman cowed, and he groaned but never wept. Nobody had seen a drop of tear in his eyes. They were dry as Sahara desert. Thus he lived ten days in excruciating pain.

Sherman was dying, and the villagers were feasting. The relatives who came from far off places to mourn Sherman's death had a hay day. At one corner of the mango grove arrangements were made for cooking and dining of the guests. Cooks were hired, and huge cauldrons were on the flames for day and night. Batches after batches dined dal, rice and smashed potato, and they were not in hurry to leave Sherman's house. Men ate, and smoked under the mango trees at noon, and in the evening they sat by the big pond. The wind blew and they felt drowsy. They wallowed on the dry leaves and gossiped about the day's highlights.

Women quarrelled and abused each other for their wanton children. The children cried and complained, and their mothers followed them in harsh tongues. They felt angry, and rushed to their men wallowing by the edges of the pond, and urged them to go home in the next morning. Morning came, and they forgot all. They as usual drank glasses of tea, gobbled dozens of bread, ate dishes of rice, and gulped gallons of water. And the children like monkeys were chattering, quarrelling, beating and crying all the time. They were found to be swinging in the branches, swimming in the pond, catching grasshoppers and butterflies, and pelting at dogs and birds and frogs.

There was a long verandah stuck to the big house. From early morning to night peasants usually sat, smoked, and gossiped there. But at summer noon it was too hot to be occupied, and the peasants made some alternative arrangement for passing the day. They then sat under the shade of a tall kadam tree. And it was the month of late June. The tree was in full bloom, and the scent wafted the entire house. For ten days rolls of wailing filled the air of Sherman's house. Whenever a new visitor came, the women already thronged at the sides of Sherman's death bed, began crying louder. With the mothers children also cried. They wailed for five minutes or so, and then the newcomer wiped her tears and soon began gossiping with other known or unknown faces. She forgot Sherman and all, and joined in the animated gossips and juicy rumours of unwed pregnant girl, elopement or theft.

So the days were passing. Peasants routinely ate and slept at Sherman's house. The beautiful white house turned into a festive ground. Villagers sighed and mourned for Sherman. Some close friends of Sherman shared anecdotes of his life. The storytelling usually took place at night, when the heat was gone, and the wind blew, and the stars shone, and the children slept. People crowded around the teller and they smoked, and pined for Sherman. At outward he looked a tough man, masculine, brave, and grave. But his heart was soft. He helped the poor peasants, and the peasants loved him too. He never did wrong to anyone in his entire life.

"Why did he take home Jarina, a young girl of barely fourteen of Abalpara?" asked a peasant, lean and pale with a scary face.

"Who asked, who asked this?" The storyteller made a survey of the faces of his audience taking a hurricane in his hand. Most of them were dozing, and he could not mark the face of the man who asked. All were silent. And he resumed, "Don't ask, only hear. Sherman was a king to us. And a king could do no wrong. Why Jarina alone? If he wished he could have married all the girls of our villages. But had he done this? And do you really know why he married Jarina. She was unmarried and was pregnant. The boy who spoilt the girl, oh, what his name..., ah, Mujahid fled to Bhutan, and never came back. And Sherman, our king, saved the girl from disgrace and shame and bestowed honour on her instead. We should be grateful to the lion-hearted man."

The peasants gaped and yawned, and said nothing. And the peasant who asked was indifferently counting the stars.

The night was dead, and the mosaic of stars canopied it. No birds sang; no insects whirred. The water of the pond was lapping still, sparkled by the shooting stars. People lay everywhere, some snoring, few dreaming, and throwing hands and legs spasmodically, and rest lay as if they were lifeless. Occasionally from distant fields foxes yelped, and dogs of Sherman were barking and whining at them back.

Thus nine days and nine nights passed and Sherman lay bedsored. People prayed for his recovery. Village maulvis recited the holy book, and the incense at the lone corner was burning and dying and burning again. Women were never tired of wailing sitting by dying bed. His wives and sons looked harried and mad. They forgot to bath, to have food or to sleep. Peasant women looked at Sherman's wives and sons with pity and they cried for them. They sighed, mourned, and cried, and cried. If children cried for going home, village women rebuked them, and offered some coins for candy. Men at times went home quickly to give fodder to cows or goats or buffaloes or to scatter grains to hens and pigeons. And soon they ran back to Sherman's.

After long summer days of scorching heat and humidity, came the night of heavy downpour. For months the sun burnt and glowed, and not a cloud sailed in the dark blue sky. People from the wee hours readied for another hot day. Ponds and marshes were dry. And the river was lean, and lost its youthful buoyancy. The columns of dust smoked the air. Peasants worked at fields in the early morning and late evening. They passed the noon under the shade of some big trees at some gardens, or lay almost naked on the mud floors of their huts.

From the afternoon dark clouds, rushing suddenly from nowhere darkened the sky. First began the dust storm. It made people almost blind. Streets and fields were empty. People rushed towards huts. The wind rushed, many tin sheds were damaged. Some tin pieces flung far, trees broken. Then the spate of the storm slowed, and lighting flashed, and clouds burst and growled, and roared and howled. Rain began to pour, and it continued whole night. Water filled the water bodies, and frogs croaked, and crickets began to sing. Golden frogs suddenly appeared everywhere, and they croaked and croaked. It filled the fresh air. At Sherman's house people huddled around his bed. The front yard and the mango grove and the pond were under knee-deep water. People enjoyed the first shower of the monsoon. The peasants were happy as their wait for the rain was over, and they could now begin ploughing fields for planting paddy seedlings

The rain didn't stop. It seemed that there was a hole in the sky over Sherman's house. Children slept wherever they found an empty space in the house, and the men and women were all dozing. The night was dark, but Sherman's house was lit with a dozen of emergency lanterns. The light fell on the faces of the rugged crowd.

Suddenly a loud roll of wailing broke the stillness of the night. Sherman was convulsing. He tried to breath, and the dry blue veins of his neck were coming out of the slackened skin. His eye balls became large and wide, as if they were coming out of the deep eye hole. His body twisted and cheeks hollowed. Minutes after, he became lifeless.

The dogs crooned long, and the foxes began squeaking in the bamboo bush. Sherman's wives and sons and in-laws were crying and berating breasts, shaking heads up and down like mad women. They clutched the dead body. And Sherman's was lying peacefully with his eyes wide open. The drowsy villagers hearing the piteous roll of mourning startled to their feet. And soon they joined Sherman's family. They wailed and wailed. When their eyes got dried and their voice choked, they sobbed and whined.

The morning was cool and calm. Children slept like logs. The sun was rising slowly. The street was empty. The trees wore a festive look, leaves washed. A group of peasants at the verandah of Sherman's house sat on haunches, and quietly smoked. Four shovels they brought. The corpse was being laid in the middle of the yard, and it would be washed by the eldest son. People lined for a last look at Sherman. Coffin was readied and it was carried to the burial ground by his sons, some five kilometer distance. Villagers sadly followed the coffin through the barren fields, and thickets. Sakina and Jarina beat breasts, and threw hands at every side. They tried to run after the coffin. But village women forcibly stopped them.

Half an hour later the coffin and the crowd entered into the burial ground. In a corner of the cemetery crows quarrelled and cawed on the branches of a kadam tree. It bore clusters of flowers, and the branches hung low with the burden of its scented flowers.

Two years passed. A caretaker looked after Sherman's house for some months. But the watchman at a moonlit night saw Sherman cheerfully rocking by his side. He swooned and turned mad at that night. The big white house now stood empty, abandoned. It was covered with leafy undergrowth. An eerie silence shrouded it. Children feared and men and women shunned its shadow.

❖❖❖